A NEW LIFE FOR ROSEMARY

Alone since the loss of her family in an air-raid, Rosemary — newly demobbed from the WRNS — returns to her old home. But she is shocked to find that a whole family has been temporarily housed there . . . With little knowledge of children and cooking, and with housework to do, she has her hands full — especially when strange things begin happening at the bottom of her garden . . . Friends help her cope, as she helps them. But will she also cope when romance calls?

Books by Anne Holman
in the Linford Romance Library:

SAIL AWAY TO LOVE
HER HEART'S DESIRE
FLYING TO HEAVEN
FINDING LOVE
HIDDEN LOVE
SECRET LOVE
CAPTURED LOVE
THE LONGMAN GIRL
THE OWNER OF THORPE HALL
THE CAPTAIN'S MESSENGER
BELLE OF THE BALL
CASSIE'S FAVOUR
THE GOLDEN DOLLY

ANNE HOLMAN

A NEW LIFE FOR ROSEMARY

Complete and Unabridged

LINFORD
Leicester

First published in Great Britain in 2006

First Linford Edition
published 2007

British Library CIP Data

Holman, Anne
    A new life for Rosemary.—Large print ed.—
Linford romance library
1. Love stories
2. Large type books
I. Title
823.9'14 [F]

ISBN 978–1–84617–986–0

Published by
F. A. Thorpe (Publishing)
Anstey, Leicestershire

Set by Words & Graphics Ltd.
Anstey, Leicestershire
Printed and bound in Great Britain by
T. J. International Ltd., Padstow, Cornwall

This book is printed on acid-free paper

Starting Afresh

Rosemary Shepherd sighed as she carried her suitcase towards the door. She felt satisfied she had left her cabin looking ship-shape, but dryness in her mouth made her swallow as she paused at the doorway, looking back nostalgically at the cabin that had been her home for so long.

The locker was empty, ready for another Wren to put in her dark blue serge skirts and jackets, white shirts, stiff collars, black tie and stockings, and highly polished black shoes.

Rosemary felt strange wearing civilian clothes. For a moment she longed to be a Leading Wren again, about to go on duty. But she couldn't. All that was over. She'd handed in her uniform and had been through demob procedures — this time she was going ashore for good.

'Do hurry up, Rosemary,' called the Wren Tilly driver, who had rushed in to fetch her, 'or you'll miss the train.'

Clutching her handbag, which contained her last travel warrant for a free ride home, Rosemary resolutely turned her back on the cabin and followed the Wren driver who was striding out of the WRNS quarters.

Outside, a chorus of cheery voices greeted her. They were all waiting to see her off.

'Goodbye, Rosemary.'

'Good luck, luv.'

'Ta-ra.'

'Take care.'

Bright-faced, laughing girls, with their blue caps perched on their heads, crowded around Rosemary, all wishing her luck. She could hardly say anything in reply as tears welled up in her eyes and spilled out, running down her cheeks, although she grinned. She was going to miss them all so much. Each and every one of them gave Rosemary a hug and she was ushered along amid cries of 'Don't forget us!' As if she could!

Even the duty Third Officer gave her a smile and a warm handshake.

Once she was seated in the Tilly, the driver shot off. Rosemary almost fell out of the vehicle as she leaned backwards to wave to her friends of the past four years.

Her mind drifted back to her school friends and she wondered what had happened to them. There was giggly Phyllis, and bossy Josephine. She smiled as she remembered Josephine's young brother Douglas, who was always getting into scrapes, climbing onto roof tops as well as up trees. And there was the older one, John, who'd become a doctor and joined the Royal Navy. All those youngsters she used to play with as a child — where were they now?

As the Tilly passed through the main gate and sped on towards the railway station, Rosemary smiled. There were some things to be thankful for. No more parades where you had to stand in a bitter wind that made your ankles ache. No more service numbers and salutes. No more eagle-eyed officers looking over your cabin for dust for you to remove . . .

Yes, there were some things she wouldn't miss.

But alas, no more laughs with the girls; no laundry service with clean collars and shirts; and no more meals provided.

Rosemary knew her life was about to start afresh, and she wasn't at all sure what was in store for her.

Sadly, she had no family to go home to. Her fiancé, a Fleet Air Arm pilot, had been killed on active service during the war, and her parents and younger sister had died in a cinema when it was bombed during an air raid.

All Rosemary had now was the old family house near Exeter. It had been locked up and was probably now full of spiders and goodness knows what else. It would certainly need a good clean. And although the war was over, people were still enduring hard times with shortages — and a harsh winter just beginning.

She was well aware that many things would have changed during her service years away — and she must also face the fact that she no longer had an income. She would need a job. But what kind of job? Her work in the WRNS, spotting aircraft by radar, wasn't going to help her find a job in Civvy Street, was it? So, what on earth was she going to do?

★ ★ ★

Rosemary's heart beat faster as she spotted Petty Officer Dennis Painter sitting on one of the station platform benches. She had no doubt in her mind that he was waiting for her. He'd sat himself not far from the ticket office, so she couldn't avoid walking past him.

In his hand was a platform ticket, and his nose was buried in *The Racing Times*. He seemed to be good at picking out winning horses, Rosemary acknowledged. He'd bought a motor-bike with his recent winnings and taken her out for a spin on it. Clearly, Dennis was a man who would go far. Once he was out of his wartime service and running his own business, which he'd told her he wanted to do, Rosemary was convinced he'd soon become a millionaire.

Seeing her, Dennis folded up his paper and leaped to his feet.

'Hi, sunshine,' he said, walking over and taking her suitcase from her, carrying it as easily as if it were filled with feathers. 'Let's go down to the far end of the platform — I'd like to be alone with my girl.'

It was kind of him to come and see her off, but she wasn't really 'his girl', Rosemary thought, with a touch of irritation. They'd gone out together a few times, and had danced at the camp dances, but Rosemary had never felt any more than friendship between them — although perhaps he did.

There was nothing she could do about it if he did, though. She was still grieving for Rob . . .

Rosemary liked lots of things about Dennis. His friendship and his willingness to take her out had helped her to overcome her loss to some extent. He could make her chuckle about the oddities of service life, and she had to admit he was very good at dancing the jitterbug. But today, in the emotional turmoil she was in, she wasn't overjoyed at having his company while waiting for the train, which could well be running late — they often were. And it was cold and draughty waiting on the platform.

Nevertheless, despite the cold weather, he had come to see her off, so she smiled at him and quipped, 'I wish your sunshine would materialise, Dennis!'

Having walked to the very end of the platform, Dennis plonked down her suitcase and turned to her with a broad wink.

'What's it like being a free spirit?' he asked cheerfully. Rosemary didn't feel like discussing her innermost thoughts with him.

'Oh, it's nice not having to bother to salute anyone any more,' she said flippantly; it was the first thing that came into her head.

'That's right — you won't be pushed around by officers any longer — '

'No,' Rosemary cut in quickly, 'that's not what I meant. I never thought I'd been pushed around in the Navy.'

Dennis's mouth twitched. 'Well, I do. I can't wait to finish with my war service and be able to do as I like.'

Rosemary looked up at his round face, which always reminded her of a pumpkin. He was, she considered, a confident man, wanting to stride out on his own — not at all like her. She'd always felt a little unsure of herself, and usually liked being told what to do.

She glanced down the platform, which was fast filling up with people. There would probably be no seats on the train, so she'd have to sit on her suitcase in the corridor — and the train would be unheated, too, she thought glumly. She pulled up the collar of her coat and shivered in anticipation.

Dennis was observing her closely, as if reading her thoughts. 'You know what's the trouble with you, don't you, Rosie?' he said suddenly, as if he'd been waiting for this moment and had made up his mind to be blunt with her. 'You're a shy little puss, and you're too good to be true. You could look a real smasher in the right clothes.'

His cheek astounded Rosemary. She'd had little choice in the utility clothing she was offered when she was demobbed. The clothes she wore were in lieu of her uniform. It was a 'take it or leave it' situation — she'd had to wear what was on offer.

'You don't know how to get what you want,' Dennis continued, seeming to ignore the fact that he was crushing her ego. 'Now, if you were to marry a man like me, I'd soon teach you how to stand up to people and get what you want.' He turned a broad, confident smile on her. 'So, how about it, gal?'

Bristling with annoyance, Rosemary closed her mouth tightly. She didn't want to have an argument with Dennis in the middle of the railway platform, but he really was the limit! At that moment, she really didn't know what she wanted out of life. A decent job, hopefully. Marriage, perhaps, one day — but if that was his idea of a marriage proposal, it certainly didn't tempt her.

How she wished the train would come.

'Oh, you're far too clever for me, Dennis!' she replied with a little laugh. 'I'm not the type to be out in front. I prefer to stand back and let others fly ahead.'

He shook his head and said scornfully, 'You were a Radar Wren, lass — one of the brightest. But you'll never have a decent life if you let others walk all over you!'

Rosemary took a deep breath.

'Dennis,' she said firmly, but with a playful lift to the corners of her mouth, 'you have a goal in life and I wish you luck with it. I'll probably have to scrub floors to earn my living now — and believe it or not, I'm happy to do that.'

'Well, second best won't do for me!' he groused.

She could have retorted that being bottom of the heap was not second best, it was simply the first step towards better things, but fortunately the sounds of the approaching steam engine interrupted what could rapidly have turned into a heated argument.

As the train ground to a halt, Rosemary and Dennis were engulfed by smoke from the engine, but he ignored it and picked up her suitcase again.

'Come on, I'll find you a seat,' he said.

Dennis did, of course. The carriage was full of people, yet within moments, Rosemary found herself squashed in between a large man in a shabby raincoat and a woman with furs that smelt of mothballs. It wasn't very comfortable but, almost disappearing between the two as she sat, Rosemary was relieved to be spared the problem of having to say any more than a formal goodbye to Dennis.

Wasn't that the best way to end their not-very-satisfactory relationship?

'Bye, Dennis.'

'I'll be in touch, sunshine. Look after yourself.'

Dennis's words caused Rosemary a slight pang of regret. She had no choice — there wasn't anyone else to look after her now. Despite her relief at escaping Dennis's well-meaning but unwelcome clutches, she couldn't help feeling sad as the train pulled out of the station, taking her away from her familiar past life to her unknown future.

★　★　★

During the long train journey home, Rosemary fought to keep her normally optimistic spirits high, although she knew the outlook for her was not promising.

One of the harshest winters had set in and from the carriage window, the passing countryside looked grey, bleak and frosty. They chugged past trees without leaves and frozen ponds. Huddles of farm animals waited patiently to be fed on the hard earth, the daylight dim and gloomy.

Instead of the naval daily orders, she now had austerity as the order of every day. The new ration book in her handbag would only buy essential foodstuffs, with few clothing coupons to get some warm winter clothes. She'd need fuel, too, to heat her freezing old house, but that was on short supply. At least scrubbing its floors would warm her up!

When she finally alighted from the train at the village station, feeling stiff and cold, Rosemary didn't expect anyone to recognise her and her spirits were once again at a low ebb.

It was a delightful surprise, therefore, to find her father's old friend there. William Clatterdove had taken off his cap and was waving to attract her attention as she stepped off the train.

'Mr Clatterdove, how nice to see you!' Rosemary greeted him, walking up to him and putting down her case. She held out her gloved hand.

'Hello, Rosemary,' he said with a warm smile of welcome as he shook her hand. 'I'm glad your train was on time — this cold weather's biting. Didn't fancy a long wait.' His breath made puffs in the cold air.

Rosemary was touched to realise he'd come to meet her. He'd obviously found out from her solicitor that she was arriving that day. It was very good of him to come out in this freezing weather.

'I expect my house will be like an iceberg,' she commented with a shiver. 'I haven't been there for years — I've always spent my leave with friends.'

'Oh, no, my dear. Dulcie Richardson and I went in a few days ago. Dulcie swept away a few cobwebs and I ordered some more coke for the kitchen range, so you'll have some heat and hot water.'

Her eyes lit up. 'Mr Clatterdove, how very kind of you!' she exclaimed. 'And Mrs Richardson, too.'

She remembered Mrs Dulcie Richardson, one of her mother's friends.

'Not at all. Let me take your case. I have my car outside to run you home.'

Rosemary hesitated. Wasn't he a little unsteady on his legs to be carrying a heavy case? He must be in his seventies by now. But she didn't like to cause offence, so she let him take the case and followed him out of the station.

His pre-war car needed to be cranked with a starting handle to get it fired, but eventually they were on their way.

'Dulcie sends you her love — she says she hopes to visit you soon,' Mr Clatterdove told her as they drove off. 'She's been looking after your parents' dog, you know.'

'You mean Hetty?' Rosemary remembered the little corgi cross dog with affection. It wasn't the prettiest animal

— but you could hardly blame it for its looks!

'Indeed. Hetty's quite settled with Dulcie. I don't know if you'll want her back . . . ' His voice sounded wistful and Rosemary cottoned on at once. Perhaps Dulcie had become so fond of the dog, she'd asked Mr Clatterdove to ask her if she could keep it?

'Oh, I wouldn't dream of taking her away from Mrs Richardson now. Hetty must be very attached to her — I don't suppose she'll remember me now anyway.'

'She will, I'm sure. Dogs are canny creatures. And you've only been away four years.'

Seemingly content to have sorted out the question of Hetty's future, Mr Clatterdove drove in silence for a while.

As they wended their way along the narrow, twisting Devon lanes, Rosemary sat viewing the landscape she'd known since she was a little girl. She felt very strange and yet pleased to be on the way to her childhood home

— and what a wonderful surprise she'd had being welcomed home by two of her parents' old neighbours. Rosemary remembered that both of them had written her kind letters after her family had been killed. It was so nice that they hadn't forgotten her.

When Rosemary's family home, High Boughs, came into sight, Mr Clatterdove glanced at her.

'Oh, Rosemary, one thing I should have mentioned earlier is that the family living in your house are — '

'What?' Rosemary's eyes widened in surprise at his words. 'I beg your pardon, Mr Clatterdove — what family?'

'Didn't you know?' He looked startled. 'It was taken over by the council housing officer looking for a temporary home for bombed-out families. The Morton family are living in part of it.'

Rosemary was astonished. 'Shouldn't I have been told?'

'Indeed you should.'

'Then why wasn't I?'

'Didn't you get a letter from your solicitor?' he asked.

Rosemary frowned. Maybe she had. Guiltily, she realised that she probably hadn't bothered to read it properly. Letters from her solicitors did arrive periodically, but they were usually boring to read, containing only a report on the estate. She'd probably intended to read it but had stuffed it away and forgotten about it — like so many other letters she should have replied to. Now she regretted that she was so bad at dealing with her correspondence. She vowed to be more careful and read her letters properly in future.

'Oh well,' she sighed. 'I suppose I would have agreed to let the family use the house anyway. How long will they be there?'

'That's anyone's guess. Families are being re-housed as fast as they can build new ones.'

'What's this family like?' Rosemary asked nervously.

'The father, Michael, is a soldier.

Abroad just now. The mother's called Dianne and her children are . . . well, you know what children are like!'

Rosemary didn't know. They didn't have children in the WRNS. They were an unknown quantity to her.

She swallowed nervously. 'How many children?'

'Two of her own and another one staying for a while. And Dianne's expecting a baby shortly.'

'Heavens! That many?' Rosemary exclaimed.

He smiled gently. 'They've been looking forward to you arriving.'

So she wasn't going home to an empty house after all, Rosemary thought wryly. Her house had been taken over by strangers. She didn't like the idea very much, but hopefully it wouldn't be for long.

Of course, she could be upset and make a fuss about the situation. But she decided she wouldn't. Like everyone who'd been caught up in the war, she'd become used to making the best of what was thrown at her.

'Well,' she said to William Clatter-dove, 'at least I won't be lonely!'

'They won't be there just now,' he said. 'They took the bus into Exeter this morning and won't be back till this evening.'

Rosemary wasn't sorry to hear this. At least she would have her house to herself for a few hours.

Meeting The Family

As the car purred up the drive — home at last — Rosemary felt a jumble of emotions flooding through her. Seeing the old house again gave her a pang of sorrow, knowing that there would be no mother, father or younger sister coming out to greet her.

Only strangers to meet later on in the day . . .

The screech of the car brakes jolted her out of her reverie.

'What's the matter?' she gasped.

'Susan's left her pedal cycle on the drive — I almost ran over it,' Mr Clatterdove exclaimed, irritated.

Sure enough, there was a child's bicycle lying on its side in the middle of the drive. Rosemary vaguely recognised it as her own old bicycle.

'You did well not to run over it,' she remarked.

He straightened the steering wheel and pulled the handbrake on fiercely.

'You'll probably find children's toys lying around all over the place,' he said. 'They've had the place to themselves.'

Rosemary felt a slight pang of regret. Yes, of course they would have found her old toy box — and helped themselves!

Still, her thoughts went on bracingly, it wasn't as though she'd be able to ride her bicycle again. And all those old toys she'd forgotten about — her doll's house and cuddly toys — well, if these children had lost all their toys in a bombing raid, it was only fair to let them enjoy playing with her old ones.

Mr Clatterdove was still talking.

'Someone's using your old outhouses too.'

'Oh?' Rosemary remembered the garage, which was situated down at the bottom of the long garden. There was also a hen house, a big timber barn and the garden shed where her father had had a workbench and kept his tools.

'Yes, I only noticed it the other day. A van was parked there, but by the time I went to investigate, whoever it was had left.'

Rosemary opened her car door to get out.

'I suppose someone noticed the opportunity for some free garaging,' she remarked. 'I'll have to turn a blind eye to what's going on.'

'No!' His shout made her jump. 'You don't have to. It's your house — you make the rules.'

'I've had enough of rules and regulations,' Rosemary told him with a smile. 'I'm a civilian now and I'm not going to go around ordering people about.'

Mr Clatterdove tutted as he clambered out of the car. 'Of course, you're free to do as you think, but some people will take advantage of you if you're not careful. You should remember criminals can lurk anywhere.'

'Criminals? In this sleepy old village?'

'There are always evil things being

done,' he warned, 'even in sleepy little villages. Human nature hasn't changed just because Hitler has been defeated. So, you just take care, my dear.'

Rosemary bent to give his wrinkled cheek a kiss. 'Thank you, Mr Clatter — '

'Call me Bill,' the old man said, patting her arm kindly.

She smiled. 'Thank you very much, Bill, for bringing me home.'

Picking her up and driving her home, she observed, had been quite an ordeal for the old man. She was touched by his kindness.

'We've all tried to do our bit while you youngsters were sent off to the Army, Navy or RAF,' he replied. 'But now we've got to help you settle back into civilian life.'

Rosemary wasn't sure that everyone leaving the services would be welcomed back with open arms as she had been.

'And ex-service people have to be willing to accept that things might not be exactly as they left them,' she replied.

He gave a short laugh. 'As you've already found, m'dear. Yes, you'll find lots of changes, Rosemary. Things are not the same. We're all trying to pick up the pieces after the war. And some youngsters have been without their parents' guidance.'

Rosemary nodded. She wouldn't be the only one with a life to straighten out.

★ ★ ★

Hours later, Rosemary sat in the warm kitchen cupping a mug of hot tea. She didn't think it wrong to help herself to a spoonful of the tea and a drop of the milk she had found as she would go down to the village store tomorrow and replace anything she'd taken.

There wasn't much else to eat in the pantry, but there was a delicious smell of cooking stew wafting from the slow oven. Of course, Dianne Morton would have made it so that her family would have a hot meal waiting for them when they returned home.

She'd explored the house from top to bottom and had found evidence of the Morton family in every room — except her own, thank goodness. It must have been locked to keep the children out.

The room was filled with mementoes of her family: photographs, ornaments and personal items which had belonged to her father, her mother, and her young sister, Belinda.

She opened her mother's red leather jewellery box and gazed at the rings, necklaces, brooches and bracelets she remembered her mother wearing. The memories flooded back as she picked up each piece one at a time to examine it closely . . .

A gleaming pearl necklace — how clearly she remembered her mother wearing it; a sparkling sapphire ring and her gold link bracelet with charms hanging on it. Some of the jewellery had belonged to her grandmother and had been passed down to her mother. Now all of it belonged to her — it was all she had left of her loving family.

She couldn't help the tears that sprang to her eyes.

Hastily drying her eyes in case the Morton family came back, she busied herself unpacking and sorting out her chest of drawers and wardrobe. She was touched to find that someone had made up her bed with clean sheets and dusted the furniture.

At last, having done all she could, Rosemary wondered why the Morton family were so late returning from Exeter. It was becoming darker by the moment outside, she thought, as she went to draw the kitchen curtains.

Just then, a light at the bottom of the garden caught her eye. Rosemary stared. It appeared to be a torchlight, moving towards the garage. A second later it was gone.

Had someone gone into her garage? Wasn't it locked? Well, no, she didn't suppose it was. People living in the village rarely locked any doors, and she remembered people even used to leave the car keys in the ignition when they popped into a shop!

A sudden rattle at the kitchen door made her jump.

'Who's there?' she tried to say but no sound came out of her mouth.

'Hello, may I come in?' The deep male voice made her eyes widen. What was a man doing prowling around?

She went to the door, but before she opened it she cleared her throat and enquired loudly, 'Who's there?'

'Dr Hythe.'

'Oh, Dr Hythe,' she repeated, opening the door so that a tall figure with powdered snow covering his hat and overcoat could be seen on the doorstep. 'Come in.'

He stepped inside, removing his hat and remarking, 'You've a nice cosy kitchen here, Miss Shepherd.'

It had been a long time since anyone had called her Miss Shepherd.

'How did you know it was me?' she asked.

He hobbled into the kitchen, placed

his case on the table and opened it.

'Well you're not Mrs Morton, so you must be Rosemary Shepherd,' he said, with a smile so bright that it startled her. 'Besides, I remember you from years ago. You were friendly with my wife, Phyllis.' He took a brown bottle from his case and handed it to her saying, 'Welcome home.'

Rosemary smiled. 'Is this a welcoming drink, then?'

He laughed heartily. 'No. But that's a good idea. Perhaps you'd like to meet up with a few old friends for a half-pint down at the pub sometime? Reminisce about old times?'

'Yes, I would, thank you,' she replied at once, surprising herself. Looking up into his blue eyes, she felt suddenly tongue-tied. She'd forgotten what a good-looking man he was, although his face showed some small scars nowadays.

He'd obviously been invalided out of the Navy; she noticed he wore a heavy boot on one foot and was limping.

'I must dash — I have several patients to call on,' he told her. 'I only came to deliver this medicine for Mrs Morton.'

'Is she unwell?'

'No, it's for one of the children — I told her I'd drop it in today.' He shut his case. 'The snow's beginning to settle and I've a long bike ride ahead of me, so I'd better be on my way.'

'That must take you hours! Don't you have a car?'

He grimaced. 'Yes, and no. It's very old and it's being repaired at the moment. New cars are hard to come by these days — even for those on essential work.'

Rosemary thought quickly. 'You could borrow Dad's old Ford.'

He paused with his hand on the doorknob, his face lighting up.

'Really?'

'Well, I assume it's still there! I only got home a few hours ago and I haven't had time to explore the garden yet. Anyway, Dr Hythe, I'll let you know if it's still in working order.'

'Many thanks.' He raised his hat and was gone, leaving his footprints in the light snow on the footpath.

★ ★ ★

Rosemary felt elated. Why, after being so tired, she should suddenly feel so alert and excited, she couldn't imagine. Unless . . .

She felt her face grow warm. Dr Hythe had always been rather a heart-throb in the village . . .

She scolded herself. What was she doing thinking about a married man like that?

Besides, she had more pressing issues to worry about. It was almost five o'clock and the Morton family still hadn't returned.

She was beginning to feel concerned about them. What on earth could have delayed them? It was snowing even more steadily as she opened the door and gazed out into the darkness flecked with snowflakes; it was as if they were back in the blackouts.

Wham! Suddenly something hit her body, sending her reeling back into the kitchen.

'What the devil . . . ?' she gasped, staggering.

Turning, she saw a thin rake of a boy wearing a blue peaked hat on his straw-coloured hair. He had rushed past her into the kitchen, carrying bulging shopping bags, one of which he emptied onto the kitchen table. It was a selection of clothes he had shaken out — and a pair of boots that looked new, which he certainly needed because she could see his were badly worn down.

He lifted up a woollen jacket and hugged it to himself, chattering in a foreign language that sounded a bit like German. All of a sudden he caught sight of Rosemary and, to her amazement, bowed to her.

'Heavens!' Rosemary muttered to herself. 'Am I dreaming? What's this urchin doing here?'

The skinny boy didn't seem per-
turbed by her presence and turned
away from her once more. He put down
the jacket, ran to the bread bin and
took out the end of a loaf. He pulled off
a huge chunk of it and began to tear at
it with his teeth as he returned to look
again at the clothes on the table.

Recovering her voice, Rosemary said,
'You should wash your hands before
eating.'

He looked at her, chewing slowly,
then put down the bread. He went to
the kitchen sink and began to wash his
hands and face.

'What's your name?' Rosemary asked
at last.

'Nicky,' he replied, burying his face
in the roller towel behind the door, then
drying his hands.

She opened her mouth to speak again
but just then the door was flung open
again and a small girl entered, covered
with snow. Wiping the snow from her
face, she beamed at Rosemary and then
proceeded to remove her woolly hat

and mittens and her coat. She dropped them all onto the floor where the snow on them began to melt.

Another young boy followed her in, wearing wet Wellington boots and carrying heavy shopping bags.

'Whew!' he said as he plonked them down on the kitchen floor. Spying Rosemary, he gave her a wide grin. 'Hello! Isn't the snow wonderful?' he said. 'We'll be able to build a snowman after tea.'

'No you won't!' said a cross female voice from the doorway. 'It's supper, bath and bedtime. You can make your snowman in the morning. Oh — hello. You must be Miss Shepherd — I'm Dianne Morton. Sorry we're so late. We missed the bus and had to take the later one.'

The family had arrived.

★ ★ ★

Rosemary was taken aback by the sudden noise which had descended on the previously quiet kitchen. The children's voices rose in excited chatter as they began to warm up.

Dianne Morton was a slim lady, although heavily pregnant, and Rosemary hurried to assist her with the heaviest shopping bags.

'Oh, thank you, Miss Shepherd. But you mustn't mind us.' As if Rosemary could ignore them! 'I'll pick up the children's clothes in a minute.'

'Sit down and rest, Mrs Morton. Would you like me to make you a cup of tea?'

'Call me Dianne, please. And yes, I'd love a cup of tea.'

And so would I, thought Rosemary, missing the naval tea-boat, as well as the NAAFI.

It was the sudden yell and loud squabbling that made Rosemary use her Leading Wren commanding voice.

'Children, that's enough! Your mother is exhausted and needs to rest. Now pick up your clothes and hang them up to dry.'

Three pairs of rather scared young eyes goggled at her as she went to the wall and began to unwind the cord to lower the clothes rack.

'Yes, Miss,' said one of the boys, and began to retrieve his coat from the floor. The girl picked up her mittens and hat and ran over to put them on the clothes rack, giving Rosemary a wary look.

'Don't just stand there. You can help too,' Rosemary said, pointing at the skinny lad who stood with the bread in his hand, gaping at her.

'Miss,' said a small voice in the sudden quietness, 'Nicky doesn't understand English very well. He's Dutch.'

A Dutch boy? Was that another paragraph in her solicitor's letter that she'd missed reading? Rosemary stifled a sigh.

During the silence, a striped tabby cat appeared from nowhere, stalked over to Rosemary and curled around her legs. Clearly it wanted feeding as well.

Rosemary's mind was in a whirl. This situation was becoming more unbearable by the minute. When she'd started out on her journey that morning, she'd thought she was coming home to peaceful, village home life, with a chance to re-adjust quietly and in her own time. As it was, she seemed to have landed in a zoo, full of strange happenings and unfamiliar creatures. She was beginning to wonder if she should have signed on in the WRNS.

Then she heard Dianne's calm voice.

'Nicky, David, Susan — listen to me. As you know, this house belongs to Miss Shepherd. You are her guests, and she wants to see you behaving sensibly. Lay the table, if you please, and I'll give you your supper.'

As the children began to do as they were told, Dianne whispered to Rosemary: 'Forgive the chaos. The children aren't usually so badly behaved.'

Guilt hit Rosemary. Dianne was pregnant, and she'd had to cope with three tired, fractious children and shopping — *and* missing the bus home.

Of course, Rosemary knew she could have the family removed. But did she want to? They needed a home as much as she did. All she required now was the same outlook she'd needed when she had gone off as an apprehensive young woman to do her war service: a touch of courage and a sense of humour. Her only real trouble just now was that she was tired and hungry.

She smiled. 'I don't think they're badly behaved, they're just children — *hungry* children!'

Dianne gave her a grateful smile as she moved towards the stove. Moments later, she was spooning out the stew onto plates.

'Sit down, Miss,' said David, pulling out a kitchen chair for Rosemary to sit on.

'I want her to sit by me,' said the little girl, pouting.

'You will all sit in your usual places, Susan. Miss Shepherd will sit at the head of the table, where Daddy sits.'

Rosemary's heart lifted as she realised the family were expecting her to join them for supper.

'Are you sure you have enough food for me?' she asked.

'Oh yes. The butcher gave me some extra meat when I told him you were expected home today. And there's plenty of potatoes, onions and carrots, and pearl barley in it to satisfy even Nicky's impossible appetite.'

As the children began to eat and talk amongst themselves, Dianne turned to Rosemary and spoke in a hushed voice.

'You must excuse Nicky's manners. He was starving, like so many of the Dutch after the war ended, and he's been brought over here to fatten him up. We went to buy him some clothes today, because he came here in rags.'

Rosemary considered briefly that she'd been feeling hungry, having had no food except breakfast all day. Her unattractive utility clothing had been criticised by Dennis, too. But to have nothing to eat for days, and only rags to wear — that was real hardship.

She smiled at the Dutch boy and felt glad that she was able to offer Nicky a temporary home.

Then she looked round at them all, tucking into the delicious stew Dianne had prepared. She was obviously a good cook, even using wartime rations, and had learned to stretch them as far as possible.

Rosemary immediately felt at home with the family.

★ ★ ★

After the meal, she insisted on doing the washing up while Dianne put the children to bed.

As the last plate was dried and put away Dianne came back into the kitchen and flopped wearily into a chair.

'You should go to bed yourself. Have a hot bath and I'll bring you a cup of cocoa,' Rosemary suggested.

Dianne wiped her hand over her

forehead wearily.

'Sounds lovely but there isn't enough hot water.'

Rosemary grimaced. The four inches of hot washing-up water allowed in wartime shouldn't have taken all there was.

'Well, have your drink first, and the water should be warm enough then.' She ran the hot water tap, holding her fingers under the flow to test it. 'It's not cold,' she said. 'You should be all right if you only run the hot tap.'

'No, Miss Shepherd, the rest of the hot water is for you,' Dianne protested.

Rosemary crossed the kitchen and stood in front of the tired-looking woman. 'Now listen,' she said firmly in her Leading Wren voice. 'You're to have a bath and go to bed. That's an order, Dianne. And by the way, my name is Rosemary. Think of me as the home help here. Leave everything to me. I'm not used to children and I'm not a good cook, but strangely, I actually enjoy scrubbing floors!'

Dianne laughed. 'All right, you win. I'm dying to put my feet up. Thanks very much — Rosemary.'

When Dianne made her way upstairs, Rosemary followed quietly to make sure she did as she was told and was pleased to hear the bathroom taps running.

Hearing the boys larking about in their room, she opened the door to find a pillow fight in progress. Taking a deep breath she used the voice she had used on the parade ground, shouting, 'Get into bed — now! I don't want to have to clear up a lot of feathers when you two have finished.'

The boys dived for their beds and hid under the covers, giggling.

'Now, not another sound or you'll both be snowmen shivering outside. Do you hear?'

'Yes, Miss Shepherd,' came a muffled reply.

She wished them goodnight, but as she turned to go downstairs she heard a child's voice pleading, 'Can I have a story, please?'

She went to the other bedroom where Susan was sitting up in bed with a book on her lap.

'Susan, your mother is very tired and is having a bath, then she must go to bed.'

'Oh.' She looked disappointed. Then, 'Can you read?'

'Just about,' Rosemary replied with a smile.

'Then please will you read me a story?' Susan asked.

Coming into what used to be her sister Belinda's room sent a pang of sorrow through Rosemary. How she wished Belinda was still alive. But here was another little girl, with the same soft curls around her sweet face, needing a bedtime story. And the story book Susan had selected was one of Belinda's favourites: Cinderella.

What else could she do? Rosemary sat down and began to read.

Long before the end of the story, the little girl lay back with her eyes closed and fell asleep.

A little later, Rosemary herself was tucked up in her bed.

She was a little apprehensive to think of what lay ahead of her tomorrow.

It had been an unexpected home-coming. Not exactly unpleasant, she admitted, but certainly not what she had foreseen.

Entertaining The Troops

Rosemary was used to being on duty early in the Navy on occasions, depending on her watch. What she wasn't used to was hearing pattering feet on the landing outside her room and hushed children's voices daring each other to knock on her door to wake her up.

'You do it!'

'No — she'll be cross with me like she was yesterday.'

'Do you think she'll make us leave her house?'

'If we wake her up, she might. She's an ogre!'

Rosemary gasped as the young voices discussed this possibility for a few minutes while she finished dressing and brushed her hair. Was she seriously — in the eyes of the children — an ogre? She knew she'd been a bit short-tempered, but only because she was nervous and worried about having the family crowding her house.

She opened the door to see the three startled children standing outside. Summoning up an un-ogre-ish smile, she wished them good morning.

The Dutch boy's accent was clear as he wailed, 'I'm hungry.'

David poked him with his elbow. 'You're always hungry, Nicky. And I don't know where all the food you eat goes to — you're as tall and thin as a giraffe!'

The children's giggles made Rosemary's smile more genuine.

'Why are you all in your nightwear?' she asked. 'Isn't it time you were dressed?'

'Miss Shepherd, we want to build a snowman, but Mum's not well,' David explained. 'And she won't let us play outside until we've had breakfast.'

The smile vanished from Rosemary's face. With Mrs Morton ill she was confronted with more than simply having three children in her house; she would have to look after them as well!

'I'd better go and see your mother,' she said, 'then we'll have breakfast.'

The children scurried back to their rooms.

'It won't take me long to get dressed,' David remarked.

'Nor me,' said Susan.

'May I put on my new boots and clothes, please?' Nicky called, his bright blue eyes sparkling in anticipation.

Rosemary paused, unsure. She was used to following orders and now she had a decision to make — a decision unlike any she'd ever had to make before. The boy was plainly eager to wear his new clothes.

At last she considered that even if Dianne told him to change back into his ragged clothes later, it would make him happy for a while, which was important for the deprived boy, so she nodded, and received a wide grin from him.

'Dank you,' he said with a bow.

She knocked softly on Dianne's bedroom door, and heard a feeble, 'Come in,' in response.

Dianne was lying on what had been Rosemary's parents' bed. She looked poorly as she tried to sit up.

'I shouldn't have gone into town yesterday — I feel washed out,' she murmured. 'I'm sorry if the children have been bothering you.'

If Rosemary were to be completely honest, having the children around *did* bother her. She would rather the Mortons were not in her home. They were a nice family, but they had certainly presented her with problems. She knew, however, that she'd just have to make the best of the situation.

She made the effort to smile. 'The children are getting dressed, then I'll get them some breakfast. Shall I bring you up a cup of tea and some toast?'

'That's very kind of you, Rosemary. But you shouldn't be waiting on me.' Dianne tried to raise herself again but fell back on her pillow with a pained sigh.

'Don't worry. Stay where you are and have a long rest today. It'll do you good.'

Dianne closed her eyes. 'But there's so much I have to do,' she fretted. 'I must make the children's porridge. And the stove'll go out if I don't take the ash out and fill it with coke.' Her voice was weary. 'I'll have to prepare some dinner, too, and give Nicky his medicine. And Matilda needs feeding — that's the cat . . . I promise you I'll get up soon — as soon as I find the strength.'

Rosemary took a deep breath. This poor woman was clearly not up to all this work in her condition.

'I can do all the things you want doing; I haven't anything else to do today.' Except, she remembered, see about her dad's car for Dr Hythe. Gosh, she was going to be busy!

Dianne didn't argue. Relief washed over her. It was all right. Rosemary could deal with things — she sounded so competent!

Little did she know that Rosemary was quaking in her boots!

The children were quarrelling when Rosemary arrived downstairs in the kitchen, arguing about the porridge they were trying to make.

'Mum doesn't make it that way, Dave!' Susan protested.

'Yes, she does,' he snapped back. 'Anyhow,' he added with a twist to his mouth, 'it'll be more or less the same.'

'I want some food,' Nicky moaned as his stomach growled.

Rosemary towered over them.

'Attention!' she called and all three turned to her, falling silent.

'Let's get organised. Susan, lay the table, if you please, and, Nicky, cut some bread. David, you can show me the saucepan your mother uses for porridge and find the oatmeal. Oh, I see you already have the packet out — although most of it's on the floor!'

Trying to remember where her mother used to keep her cookery books, or a recipe for making porridge, her thoughts were interrupted by a cry from Susan.

'The milkman's coming!'

Glad of this reprieve, Rosemary opened the kitchen door and saw a man driving a pony and a cart filled with metal milk churns. He halted, jumped off the milk float and then filled three small metal cans, which he brought over to her, whistling cheerfully.

'Morning, ma'am.' He beamed, handing her the milk cans.

'Good morning to you, Sid.'

He did a double-take.

'Why, if it isn't Rosemary Shepherd! Blow me! You've grown up, young lady. You look just like your ma, God rest her soul.'

Rosemary smiled, delighted — her mother had been renowned for being an attractive woman.

'Are you able to give us any extra milk today, please?' she asked.

Sid said he would fetch some more and while she waited for him to return with an extra can, Rosemary surveyed the snow.

'Is there a lot of snow about today?' she asked him.

'Only here and there. But it's icy. This is the worst winter I can remember.'

'I need to get my father's car out of the garage and working for Dr Hythe to use,' Rosemary said. 'His car has broken down. Can you suggest who could help me?'

Sid scratched his eyebrow.

'The garage is at the end of the village, but you need a man who knows a little about starting old cars. My son Bert's quite handy at that sort of thing. Shall I ask him to call round?'

'Yes, please do.'

'Will do.'

As he turned to leave, Rosemary hissed in his ear, 'Sid, do you know how to make porridge?'

'For this lot?' He smiled widely, jerking his thumb at the children, and Rosemary smiled ruefully and nodded.

'I didn't learn to cook in the Wrens.'

In a quiet voice he told her how it

was made, and after a trip back to his float, he returned with a very small carton of cream.

'This'll cost you thruppence. Put it on top the porridge and they'll love it, even if it ain't cooked quite right.'

He went back to whistling loudly as he set his pony off again.

The porridge was a hit with the children.

'You're a good cook, Miss Shepherd,' said Susan, which made Rosemary chuckle.

★ ★ ★

After being wrapped up in their coats, scarves, hats but no gloves the children were let outside to spend their energy making a snowman in the garden, while she took a cup of tea and a small bowl of creamy porridge upstairs to Dianne.

Dianne was full of apologies. 'Sorry to be so useless,' she said.

'Heavens, Dianne, you're pregnant, and you can't help feeling worn out after your trek into Exeter yesterday in that bitter weather. Here, get this hot porridge down you.'

'Are the children behaving?' Dianne asked anxiously.

'They daren't not behave!'

'You're marvellous, Rosemary — a real angel!'

'Well, the children think I'm an ogre.' Rosemary laughed. 'And this angel can't cook. So how do I get dinner ready?'

Fortified by her breakfast, Dianne sat up.

'I bought some mince yesterday. It's in the larder. Put it in the frying-pan and fry it very gently, then cut an onion up — cut it very small, though, because Susan won't eat onions . . . '

Fortunately cottage pie didn't seem too complicated to make. Heading downstairs again with an empty cup and bowl, Rosemary felt a glow of achievement. Dianne had made her feel needed and far more capable than she felt.

The children had built their snow-man and their cheeks were pink as they crowded into the kitchen and persuaded her to come and take a look at it.

As she admired their rather squashy effort, her mind was on coming up with some other amusement for them.

'I think there may be a sledge in the garage,' she told them. 'My dad made it for my sister and me when we were young.'

The children jumped up and down in excitement when they were given permission to look for the sledge and handed the rusty key for the garage.

★ ★ ★

Hours later, seated around the kitchen table, Rosemary reflected on how her life had changed in just thirty-six hours. Although she'd worked just as hard in the Wrens, there had always come a time when her stint was over and she could go off duty. Here, there was no off duty in sight.

The meal was well underway and when Susan remarked that it was the best cottage pie she'd ever tasted because there was no onion in it, Rosemary smiled; talk about fooling the enemy!

She heard all about the excitement they'd had with the old sledge, and smiled indulgently until she became aware of Susan raising her voice in argument.

'There *was* a man there! I've seen him before.'

Rosemary's attention was drawn to listen to the chatter.

'You make up stories!' said David to his sister.

'No, I don't.'

Rosemary tapped the end of her fork on the wooden table-top.

'What are you talking about?'

David put down his fork.

'It's just Susan making up stories, Miss Shepherd. When we went to find the sledge, Susan said she saw a man running away from the barn. I said she didn't.'

'I did,' said the five-year-old stubbornly. 'I did, I did, I did.'

Nicky picked up his empty plate and licked it.

'I saw some footprints in the snow. Many men have been in the barn,' he said.

Rosemary was about to tell him not to lick his plate clean, but instead she asked, 'What were they doing in there?'

'Playing?' suggested Susan.

'With all those boxes? Don't be stupid, Susan.'

Boxes? Rosemary sighed. She would have to take a look round those outhouses herself. She had intended to anyhow, but she'd been very busy all morning. Bill Clatterdove had called round with a cabbage from his garden and told her Dulcie Richardson had got some burst pipes and he was off to find a plumber for her. The baker's van had come, and she'd had to run upstairs to ask Dianne how many loaves they'd need for the week.

What with these interruptions on top of the cooking and cleaning, she'd hardly had time to make a cup of tea for Dianne.

So much for quiet country living, she thought ruefully.

Supervising the children washing up after lunch took so long, Rosemary began to think it would be teatime before they finished. She would have been quicker doing it herself. At first they argued that they never had to wash up, but she insisted they helped. She had to be patient and make sure they learned to do it properly.

As their coats and hats were soaked, they couldn't go out again until they'd dried overnight, so she sent them upstairs to play in their rooms until teatime, promising that they could listen to Children's Hour on the wireless afterwards.

★　★　★

Rosemary was unsettled. Bill Clatterdove had told her that he had the impression someone was using her outhouses, and now the children had mentioned boxes in the barn. She'd seen that light down at the bottom of the garden at night, too. What was going on? She knew she would have to investigate.

It was bitterly cold and would be getting dark soon, so she wasted no time. Putting on her coat and lifting the collar, she shoved her hands in her pockets. A biting wind whirled around her as she hurried down the path towards the outhouses.

At first sight there appeared to be no-one about. The old buildings had been neglected since her father had died. The paint was peeling and she heard a wood-slatted door rattling in the wind. An old sack covering the outside taps was flapping wildly.

Looking down at the ground, she could see there were hundreds of footprints where the children had been running around.

Then she noticed a faint light coming

from inside the garage. Someone was in there!

'Well,' she told herself, 'it's my garage so I'd better go and see.'

Wishing she'd brought a torch, she proceeded with cautious steps up to the garage window and peered in. Cobwebs prevented her from seeing clearly, but a faint light was visible.

Creeping around to the front of the garage she saw the door was ajar.

Then she heard the quiet whistling — the same tune the milkman had been whistling that morning!

'Hello, Miss,' came a cheerful voice from inside the garage.

Rosemary gasped. 'Oh, Sid, you gave me a fright!'

'I'm Bert, Miss. My dad said you wanted your car checked over and as I was coming down the lane I popped in to take a look at it. It'll be too dark to see a bloomin' thing in here soon.'

'That's very kind of you, Bert,' said Rosemary.

Stepping nearer, she saw how alike

father and son were.

The car bonnet was up and Bert was examining the engine with his torch.

'Will it go?' she asked at last.

Bert grinned, wiping his dirty hands on a dirtier piece of cloth.

'There's plenty of life in the old girl yet!'

Relief washed over her.

'What needs doing to it?'

'It's a good thing someone had the sense to take the wheels off and put the car up on bricks. It means the wheels can go on again, then a run round with the oil can and a tank of petrol should see her safely on the road.'

'That sounds splendid.'

Bert's blackened face grinned at her.

'It would be — if you could get petrol.'

Rosemary's face fell.

'Can't you buy it?' she asked helplessly.

'Only on the black market.'

'Oh.'

'You'll have to apply for petrol

coupons — but not everyone gets them.'

Rosemary thought for a moment.

'I expect Dr Hythe does. I'll ring him. Thanks ever so much for coming Bert.'

Back in the house, she phoned the doctor right away.

'This is Rosemary Shepherd. You'll be pleased to hear that my father's old car is still going strong.'

'That is good news.' His deep voice was a joy to hear.

'So you can pick it up whenever you like. But it will need petrol.'

'May I come round in the morning? Very early, I'm afraid. I'll bring a can of petrol and then take her to the garage to fill her up.'

'I'll have the car key ready for you.'

'It's very good of you.'

'Oh, Dr Hythe — '

'John, please — we're old friends, after all.'

She was taken aback. 'Well, yes, we were, as children.'

'I'd like to think we still are.'

'Right — er — John, then. Mrs Morton is in bed, exhausted after her shopping expedition into Exeter yesterday. I haven't really had time to talk to her much. Is her baby due soon?'

'It is — although babies have a habit of coming when they choose to, not when we plan for them. Is she in any pain?'

'She hasn't mentioned she's in pain — only very tired.'

'Well then, if she's comfortable and warm in bed, let her stay there. I'll pop in tomorrow morning and see her. But if you're worried about her, call me — even if it's midnight.'

As Rosemary hung up, it occurred to her that she couldn't think of a nicer person to lend her father's car to than Dr John Hythe.

★　★　★

It was much later that evening, after the children had gone to bed, that Rosemary remembered she hadn't had a

63

look to see if there were any boxes in the barn.

Venturing out at this time of night — even down to the bottom of the garden — wasn't an inviting prospect, but she told herself that many people had an outside toilet and had no choice. So, letting herself quietly out of the kitchen door, so as not to disturb the Mortons, she crunched through some freshly-fallen snow down the garden path.

Carrying a torch this time, she shone it quickly in the barn, hoping to find nothing.

But she was astounded by what she found.

Worry For Rosemary

John Hythe found himself smiling at the thought of seeing Rosemary as he dragged his bicycle out of the garden shed early the next morning.

Meeting his childhood friend again had brightened his life a little — he'd always liked Rosemary's cheerful spirit.

Seeing what an attractive woman she'd grown into, he wasn't surprised to hear that she'd been engaged to be married. Like him, though, she'd suffered the death of her loved one.

His heart constricted at the thought of his beloved wife, Phyllis, taken from him by illness at such a young age.

He sighed. Even as he'd been trying to come to terms with his loss, he'd suffered a crushed foot in his wartime service in the Navy, which had left him lame.

Now there was nothing left in his life

but his work, and he dedicated himself entirely to caring for his patients.

The war years had knocked him hard — as it had Rosemary, which gave him another reason to feel a rapport with her.

He admired her spirit, facing up to life as bravely as she did, after her whole family had been killed in the bombings.

As he cycled along in the dark that frosty morning to pick up her car which she had so kindly and readily offered to lend him, he had to be careful not to slip on the patches of black ice on the road.

With the heavy petrol can strapped behind him on the cycle's carrier and his medical bag in the front basket, it made his bicycle difficult to handle and his lights flickered more than once as he rode over the sometimes uneven country roads.

His thoughts still on Rosemary, he remembered how she'd let the other children boss her about too much when she was young and chuckled as he thought of her having to cope with the Morton family. She would have to assert herself now, but her years in the WRNS should help her do it. The Mortons were, fortunately, extremely nice people.

Arriving at last at Rosemary's house, he dismounted with relief, puffing from his ride up the hill. At once he noticed the garage doors were open, so he propped his bike against the garage wall. However, when he shone his torch into the garage, he stopped short in surprise. It was empty. The car wasn't here!

Now he was in a dilemma. It was still very early in the morning. He didn't want to have to go to the house and ring the doorbell — it was too early to wake up the family.

He wondered which room Rosemary slept in.

Rosemary had lain awake most of the night worrying about what she'd found in her barn. What was all that stuff doing there?

Dianne was feeling better, but Rosemary didn't want to worry her by telling her about it. She hadn't mentioned it to the children either, but they might question her about it, so she couldn't just ignore the problem and hope it would go away.

Someone had been using her barn to store goods in old tea chests. Not just a few old tea chests, either — there were piles of them!

It was bad enough that they were being stored there without her permission, but even worse was what they contained: silk stockings, shoes, coats, butter, sugar and tea — all rationed items.

Obviously her barn was being used to store black market goods.

She didn't think that going to the police was a safe option. Not knowing who might be watching the house, she was nervous about who might harm the Morton children if she reported what she'd found. Maybe if she kept quiet, the thieves would realise she was back in the house and they would move the goods away.

But wasn't it her duty to tell the authorities? Her troubled thoughts went on and on . . .

The sudden crack on the window made her sit up. Another ping and her eyes widened. Had those black marketeers come to find her? Oh dear, how she wished she was snug in her cabin back in Wrens quarters . . .

She held her breath until she thought she heard someone softly calling her name.

'Rosemary!'

It came again. Yes, it was unmistakable.

Sliding out of bed, she drew back the curtain and looked outside. There was someone out there with a torch.

Heart hammering, she opened the window a fraction.

'Who is it?' she called.

'It's John.'

John? Of course, John Hythe come to collect the car. What was the problem?

'The keys are in the ignition,' she called in a hushed voice.

'The car isn't in the garage.'

She was horrified. She'd been stupid to leave the keys in the car; it was just the sort of thing she'd always told her mother not to do! With those spivs using the barn, it had been a silly thing to do. It was no excuse to say that she'd been so tired and upset last night that she'd thought it was a good idea to leave the car keys in the ignition ready for John in the morning. She'd just made it easy for the black marketeers to drive off with it.

Opening the window further, and shivering with cold, she called, 'John, wait, I'll come down.'

Grabbing her dressing-gown and slipping her feet into her slippers, she was downstairs in an instant to let the doctor in.

'I'm so sorry. I shouldn't have left the keys in the car — '

'Indeed not!'

He could be forgiven for being put

out, she thought, having cycled all the way up to her house only to find his promised transport missing.

She went pink. 'It was stupid of me . . . I never thought . . . '

She remembered how Bill Clatterdove had warned her that she would find things had changed since the war. People were desperate for new cars, and leaving one ready for a thief to get into and drive off was madness.

'I'm sorry — '

John shrugged 'I'm sorry too; I didn't mean to snap. I'm just disappointed. I'll have to cycle over to Longbridge I suppose. But I'm fit and healthy, so it won't kill me.'

Rosemary looked at his dejected face. He was hardworking and caring. It couldn't be easy having to cycle around the countryside to see his patients.

Feeling a surge of sympathy for him, she leaned forward and kissed his cold cheek. His face broke into a smile.

'Will you have a hot cup of tea before you go?' she suggested.

Having a quiet chat in the warm kitchen calmed them both.

'I'll have to go to the police and report the car stolen,' Rosemary said with reluctance. '*And* that I have black market stuff being stored in the barn.'

John chuckled. 'I never thought you'd get mixed up with criminals!'

'I'm not!' she protested, and they laughed together. It helped to be sharing her problems with such a sympathetic listener.

When they'd finished their tea, John stood up to leave.

'I'm really sorry about the car,' Rosemary repeated. 'What will you do about transport now?'

'I've been offered a Jeep until my new car comes.'

'That'll be draughty!'

'No more than a bike — and it's faster. Thanks for the tea.' Putting on his scarf, hat and gloves, he smiled at her. 'Oh, while I remember, how is Mrs Morton?'

'Last night she seemed better. The

rest did her good.'

'That's fine for her, but you've been landed with all her work.'

She grinned. 'I have. But . . . ' She paused, then added, 'To be honest, I resented the Morton family being here at first, but I feel differently now. I like them. They're like a new family for me, if you know what I mean.'

'Yes, I think I do.' He looked searchingly into her hazel eyes. 'But they won't be here for ever.'

Embarrassed by his scrutiny, Rosemary blurted out what she'd been thinking. 'I need a job, John, if you hear of anything I could do. Mind you, I'm not skilled at anything except radar spotting!'

'You would make a good wife and mother,' he observed.

She smiled sadly. He must know she'd lost Rob . . .

'Well, I'm getting some practice at being a housewife. I've even learned to make porridge.'

'Well, that's a good start. Don't they

say the way to a man's heart is through his stomach?'

They both laughed and he turned to the door reluctantly.

'Take care,' she said, seeing him out.

'You, too,' he said, giving her a smile that warmed her to her toes.

When he'd gone she debated whether to go back to bed. The kitchen was cosy and warm. Perhaps she should just get on with some of her chores, now that she was up . . .

A sharp knock at the door made her jump. Who on earth was that?

It was John again.

'The car's back in the garage!' he declared. 'With the keys!'

'Well, I never! Where do you think it's been?'

'I've no idea — but may I use it?'

'Of course.'

He was off before she could say any more.

She poured herself another cup of tea and sat wondering at the strangeness of the situation. What on earth was going on? Why would a missing car suddenly turn up again? She sighed. And she could hardly avoid going to the police about the black market boxes now that she'd told him about it, could she?

★ ★ ★

When Dianne came downstairs for breakfast, she was looking quite well, although Rosemary knew she should still take it easy.

'Just tell me what has to be done and I'll get on with it,' she assured Dianne as the children came clattering down the stairs, hungry for their breakfast.

'I've a treat for you today,' said Dianne, stirring a saucepan on the stove. 'Scrambled eggs for breakfast.'

'Mum, why are you putting powdered milk in the eggs?' David asked.

'To eke them out a bit, dear. We're still on rations, aren't we?'

David soon scraped his plate clean, saying, 'I'd love to have an egg every day for breakfast.'

'My father used to keep chickens,' Rosemary chipped in. 'The hen house is still down there in the garden.'

'Why don't you keep chickens?' Susan asked eagerly.

'Because hens need a shed so that foxes don't get them at night,' said Rosemary, 'and mine needs repairing. The chicken wire needs mending too. And birds need plenty of clean straw and corn to eat — which we haven't got.'

'My grandfather kept hens also,' Nicky put in.

'Well, we've no time to talk about hens just now,' Dianne said. 'School day today, so off you go — shoes and coats on.'

★ ★ ★

Later that day, just as Rosemary had finished scrubbing the kitchen floor, the phone rang. Knowing that Dianne would answer it, she continued with her task. She put a walkway of sheets of newspaper over the wet floor, then rinsed the prickly scrubbing brush. She put it with the hard bar of soap to dry and emptied the dirty soapy water down the sink.

'It's the doctor for you,' called Dianne.

Hoping her car hadn't broken down, Rosemary went to the phone.

'Hello, John,' she said.

'You sound breathless.'

'I've been on my hands and knees scrubbing floors.'

'Really?'

'Honestly. I love housework.'

'Well, that makes it easier for me,' he said happily, 'because I've found a job for you — and it involves housework.'

Rosemary listened as he explained how several of his older patients needed domestic help. Some would be able to pay her more than others, depending on their circumstances.

'So, what do you think?' he asked.

Rosemary had been thinking as he'd rattled off the sorts of tasks these people needed doing. It would involve shopping, cleaning, changing bedclothes for the laundry, giving medicines and lots of other household tasks. There was nothing there she couldn't cope with.

'OK, I'll give it a go,' she said.

'Good for you. Now, the first lady I know who needs help is Mrs Dulcie Richardson. She had a fall on the ice yesterday when she was taking her dog for a walk.'

'Oh, poor thing. Is she badly hurt?'

'Cuts and bruises, and she's sprained her wrist.'

'I'll pop round and see her,' Rosemary said, wondering if her old bicycle was still in the shed and in working order.

Dianne was making pastry when Rosemary went to explain to her what she was going to do. She didn't seem to mind being left alone.

'You can use my bike if yours isn't up to scratch,' she offered. 'Would you like to have tea with us when the children get back from school? Or is it too early for your evening meal?'

'No, that suits me, thanks,' said Rosemary. 'See you later.'

★   ★   ★

It didn't take her long to cycle to Mrs Richardson's. She had just dismounted and pushed her bike up to the gate when she heard furious barking coming from inside the cottage.

'Hetty,' Rosemary said to herself with a smile. 'She always was a yappy little dog.'

She knocked on the front door and opened it, calling, 'Mrs Richardson, hello! It's me, Rosemary Shepherd.'

Hetty came hurtling towards her and Rosemary knelt to embrace the little dog. Hetty obviously remembered her.

'Come in, m'dear,' Mrs Richardson called.

Rosemary went in to the front room to see her mother's old friend. She recognised the lady's face, a little more wrinkled now but with eyes as merry as ever.

'It is nice to see you again, Rosemary. I'm sorry I can't get up easily, but I hurt my arm yesterday morning after a fall. The doctor says I must rest it.'

Rosemary made Mrs Richardson some tea and sandwiches for her supper and took a stone hot water bottle up to warm her bed, wrapping her nightie around it for a cosy treat.

'You have my phone number if you need any help,' said Rosemary before she left. 'I'll be in tomorrow about nine to clean up and do any shopping you want.'

'Thank you, dear. You've cheered me up no end. But I'm worried about Hetty,' said Dulcie. 'I can't walk her or put her bowl down to feed her.'

Rosemary thought for a moment.

'I could take her back with me for the night,' she suggested. 'That'll give her a walk. Dianne will feed her, and the children will love having her overnight. Then I'll walk her back tomorrow, and you can have her during the day.'

'I'll miss not having her here tonight,'

Dulcie sounded a little sad, 'but it's for the best — and she is your dog, after all.'

'Oh, no,' Rosemary protested, 'she *used* to be our dog. Now she's yours.'

'We'll share her then,' said Dulcie, pleased.

David and Susan were thrilled to have the dog. They found a box to put by the range and placed Hetty's old blanket in it to keep her warm at night. They pestered their mother to feed her but Dianne said they must wait until after tea in case there were any scraps left.

'I'll leave Hetty some scraps,' said David.

'So will I,' said Susan. 'I want to feed the doggy.'

Hurrying upstairs, Rosemary had a quick wash and brushed her hair, humming contentedly to herself. However, she stopped abruptly when she noticed her jewel case was open.

'Did I leave it open?' she wondered, though it would be very unlike her.

Then, as she went to close it, she stopped short in shock — some of her jewellery was missing!

Her pearl necklace and sapphire ring had disappeared — and her gold link charm bracelet had gone as well!

She felt sick. Who could have come into her room and taken her family heirlooms? The children? Well, if they thought it was a good game, they would soon learn otherwise!

Of course, she told herself as she came downstairs, trying to remain calm, she didn't know for sure that it *was* them, and she prepared herself to ask them politely.

However, when she entered the kitchen, there was another shock in store. The Morton family were upset: Nicky hadn't come home from school . . .

So Much To Do

Rosemary looked at Dianne's worried face and her heart sank. She didn't like to mention that not only had the Dutch boy gone, but so had her jewellery! Not that it was very costly, but it was valuable to her. It had been safely locked in the house all the years she was in the Wrens — and even when the Mortons had come a few months ago and used the household things, no one had touched her private belongings stored in her room.

Of course, she acknowledged, since she'd come home she'd had the jewellery box out on her dressing table. It hadn't occurred to her that anyone might take anything.

She didn't like to link Nicky's disappearance with the missing jewels. That would be hinting at accusing him and she didn't know the facts.

'I expect Nicky's playing with some older boys and has forgotten the time,' she said calmly. 'He'll be in soon I'm sure. Now, I think that since the meal is ready, we should all have it and put a serving for him in the slow oven to keep warm.'

But no one really enjoyed the meal, knowing Nicky was still out there in the cold weather and the growing darkness. The gangly Dutch boy was much loved by them all. Even Hetty retired to her box, seeming to sense that everyone was worried.

By the end of the meal Nicky had still not returned, and having cleared the plates from the table, Rosemary came to a decision.

'Dianne, you should stay in the warm with the children — I'll go out and see if there's any sign of him.'

She had in mind to cycle around the village in case the lad had lost his way home, although it seemed unlikely. But someone may have seen him.

Putting on her overcoat and beret,

she wound her long scarf around her neck and put on her gloves.

Outside, it was bitterly cold and she stomped her feet briskly as she headed towards the shed. Suddenly she stopped short as she heard a tapping noise. What was that?

There it was again! It was coming from the direction of the hen house.

Gingerly she moved towards the noise and almost jumped out of her skin with fright as a furious squawking erupted nearby.

The loud squawks were followed by the angry clucking of a disturbed bird. There was a hen in the garden! It must have escaped from the nearby farm.

To her astonishment, when she looked around to see where it was, she saw Nicky had caught it!

He beamed at her. 'I have a hen to give us plenty eggs!' he announced cheerfully. 'I mend the hen house for her. You come and see how I mend it? I want to give present to everyone.'

Rosemary was taken aback. How had he got hold of a hen? Had he stolen it? She felt like scolding him for making everyone so worried about his non-appearance, but what a very kind thing he'd tried to do. He had seen that the family needed more eggs, and had made an effort to provide some.

'That's very kind of you, Nicky,' she said warmly.

'Come and see,' he said, 'I've almost finished.'

The last thing Rosemary had expected to be doing was helping repair the hen house as darkness fell. But she was amazed to see how handy Nicky had been. He'd found her father's hammer and some nails and had managed to patch up the biggest holes in the roof and sides. He'd found a little straw and pulled some long grass from the overgrown garden to make a nest for the bird.

'What about food and water?' Rosemary asked, looking at the contented hen perched on her new nest.

'I have some corn the farmer gave

me,' he said, taking a handful from his jacket pocket.

'That's not enough,' said Rosemary.

'Tomorrow I get more.'

Nicky obviously knew more about poultry than she did, so she didn't question him further, but made a mental note to see the farmer to sort out what she owed him.

They pushed the old shed door closed and left the hen safely inside.

'Come quickly now, Nicky, and have your supper.'

At the promise of food, the Dutch boy grabbed her father's tools and ran off to return them to the gardening shed. Rosemary was impressed that he didn't just leave them out. The war years had obviously made the boy diligent about looking after everything.

It was as they walked back to the house that she glanced back and saw a light in the barn. Not wishing to alarm Nicky, she said nothing. But who was it? Was it John returning her car? Or was it those shady characters making use of her barn for storing their illicit goods? She didn't feel brave enough to go and see.

The younger children were already being put to bed when they arrived in the kitchen. Rosemary took Nicky's meal out of the oven, and while he was tucking into the food, she went upstairs to tell them the good news.

'All's well. Nicky is back, safe and sound,' she announced.

'Thank God for that!' exclaimed Dianne.

'Where has he been?' David asked.

'He'll tell you when he comes up,' said their mother, 'but remember he's older than you so he can stay up later if he wants to.'

Just then, there was the thunder of footsteps on the stairs.

'I'm here,' said Nicky triumphantly.

The clamour of the three children's excited voices made Dianne wink at Rosemary.

'I think we'll leave them to it,' she said. 'Let's go and have a cup of tea, and you can tell me what he's been up to.'

'You may well need that cuppa when you hear what he's been doing,' said Rosemary with a chuckle.

Fortunately Dianne understood that Nicky was trying to be helpful by getting the hen.

'He seems to know what hens want,' said Rosemary, 'so we could probably manage to keep it if the farmer's happy about it, and if he can provide the bedding and feed for it.'

'He's a good boy,' said Dianne, holding her cup of tea with both hands. 'I don't think I could have managed him if he'd been a difficult child. I feel weighed down at present.'

'Indeed you are!' exclaimed Rosemary, looking at the other's bulging tummy, and they both laughed.

'You've been so kind to us,' said Dianne, 'providing us with a lovely home. The children all think you're wonderful, you know. And they tell me you make better porridge than I do.'

'I must say I'm quite enjoying learning to cook,' Rosemary admitted, 'so let me help you.'

'I'd be glad to have some help,' Dianne agreed.

'Mind you, since I've been home I've found I've been extraordinarily busy. And now that John has — '

'John?'

'John Hythe. You know — the doctor. We've been friends since we were young,' she added, and saw Dianne smile knowingly.

Rosemary had told the other woman about her fiancé being killed and Dianne, knowing her companion was fancy free, couldn't help speculating about her and the widower doctor.

★ ★ ★

It wasn't until she was dressing the following day that Rosemary remembered about her missing jewellery.

'I'll have to go to the police,' she told her reflection as she combed her hair at the mirror, 'and I must also speak to the farmer about Nicky's hen. I'll walk to Dulcie's cottage with Hetty and see how she is, then pick Hetty up again in the late afternoon.'

Another busy day ahead.

'Miss Shepherd, Miss Shepherd!' There was a loud banging on her bedroom door and Rosemary flung it open.

'What's the matter?' She looked down at Susan, whose eyes were wide with alarm.

'Hetty's chasing Nicky's hen around the garden.'

Oh no! It was fun for Hetty — but not for the poor hen.

Rosemary tore downstairs and out into the perishingly cold garden, grabbing the dog's collar and lead as she went. Hearing the boys' voices as well as Hetty's barking, she ran until she saw the dog facing the coal bunker and yapping at the hen, which was squawking indignantly and stalking about on top of the bunker.

'Hetty, come here!' she yelled.

The little dog turned and came running over. As she put on its collar and lead, Rosemary didn't know whether to praise it for obeying, or to scold it for pestering the hen.

Nicky ran to pick up his ruffled hen, and the children crowded around, sympathising with the distressed bird.

'You should smack that dog,' David remarked.

'Yes, you should,' Susan agreed.

Rosemary looked down at the small dog, whose soulful eyes told her the animal knew she was in trouble.

'No,' she said, 'Hetty was only doing what dogs will do if given half a chance. But we must get some chicken wire to protect the hen from dogs — and foxes.'

The children were satisfied with that and Rosemary wished all her other problems would be solved so easily.

Dianne didn't appear for breakfast, so Rosemary set to and made some porridge, glad that Sid the milkman arrived in time for her to get some more cream — her secret ingredient for making 'best-in-the-world' porridge, as the children called it.

She spoke to Nicky before the children set off for school.

'Don't worry about your hen — I'll see the farmer and make sure she has all she needs. And I'll get some chicken wire so that Hetty can't worry her again. Now off you go to school and don't go bringing back a cow this time, will you?'

Nicky had difficulty understanding what Rosemary meant at first, but as David explained it, he laughed and gave her a kiss before he went happily off to school.

Once they'd left, she set about making breakfast for Dianne.

'I'm so sorry to be leaving everything to you,' Dianne said, sitting up in bed. 'I just don't have the energy just now . . . '

'You just have to think about your baby,' Rosemary said, placing the tray carefully on the bed.

'I don't know what I'd do without you,' Dianne said warmly.

Rosemary told Dianne about her proposed busy morning, and asked what she had to do to prepare for their lunch and the children's supper.

By the time Dianne had finished, Rosemary's head was reeling and she wondered if she would be able to fit in all she had to do *and* remember all the instructions.

As she went downstairs, she couldn't help thinking how much easier her life had been as a Wren. However, she felt she had an important and challenging job to do right here.

Planning her day, she decided her first task was to take Hetty home to Dulcie.

The dog promptly curled up in her basket and fell fast asleep.

'I don't think you need worry about exercising her, Mrs Richardson,' Rosemary remarked with a smile. She decided not to tell the old lady about

Hetty's bad behaviour.

'Oh, as long as she's here with me, I'm happy,' Dulcie said.

★ ★ ★

Having so many jobs to do, it was much later that morning when Rosemary rode into the farmyard, her bicycle wheels crunching on the frozen mud in the yard. The cows looked at her with interest, breathing white clouds into the cold air. The farm border collie dogs came up barking, to sniff at her.

'Miss Shepherd, isn't it?' Mr Hunt, the farmer, came out of the dairy to greet her. 'I 'eard you were back 'ome. Now, what can I do for you, m'dear?'

'Hens,' said Rosemary. 'What can you tell me about hens?'

He laughed. 'That Dutch lad was very insistent I gave him one. But he seemed to know what fowl need.'

'Did he pay you?' Rosemary asked tentatively.

'A few Dutch coins.'

'Oh dear!'

'Don't worry. If you agree, I think he should have a small flock. Say four?'

Rosemary grimaced. Nicky's hens were going to cost her a fortune! However, she couldn't refuse and disappoint the Dutch lad when he had tried so hard to help, could she?

There was a lot to learn about hens and it was some time before all her questions were answered. Mr Hunt suggested they needed a moveable pen to keep the dog out. He and his land girls were too busy to give her a hand with putting up chicken wire to make the pen, but he promised to deliver some on his tractor, and to provide a sackful of corn and more straw for bedding.

'Make sure you store the corn somewhere where the mice can't get at it,' he added.

She racked her brain to think where it would be protected. She soon came up with the answer — she could use the coal bunker.

*   *   *

The phone was ringing when Rosemary arrived back in the house.

'Rosemary Shepherd,' she answered.

'Hello, sunshine!' a voice said cheerily.

Dennis Painter, she thought, somewhat disappointed, wondering what he wanted.

'Rosie?'

'I'm still here.'

'Are you lonely? Would you like to come over this weekend? I could take you out for a pie and a pint.'

Rosemary blinked. Lonely? Was he kidding?

'No, Dennis. I've been up since the crack of dawn dealing with a dog chasing a hen, and making breakfast for three children, one of whom is Dutch. Oh, and breakfast for their mum, who's pregnant. Then I had to do the washing up, and after that I went to see an old lady who's sprained her wrist so I have to look after her dog — the same one who was chasing the hen.

'Then on the way back I had to see a farmer about some chicken wire. And as soon as you ring off, I have to get on my bike and ride down to the local policeman's house to report a burglary.

'So I don't think you can say I've much time to be lonely, would you?'

Dennis's silence clearly indicated that he was flabbergasted. But then, that was what she had intended. He had been used to dominating her, but she was making it quite clear that she had fallen on her feet and didn't need his help any more.

He had phoned, she presumed, because *he* was the lonely one, not her.

'Rosie, that sounds — it sounds — ' he began to bluster. 'You seem overwhelmed with things. I'd better come and sort you out. I have a new motorcycle to show you anyway.'

Rosemary gave an involuntary shudder. She wasn't interested in motorcycles. She would rather have a ride with John in his Jeep.

'No, thank you, Dennis. I can't possibly . . . ' She was going to say 'cope with you as well as everything else,' but realised that would sound rude, so instead she said, 'Perhaps another weekend when I'm not so busy? I must dash, Dennis — I can hear Dianne calling me. Bye!'

Dianne was indeed calling her. Urgently.

An Exciting Time

'The baby . . . ' Dianne gasped, her face chalk-white. 'It's coming.'

Rosemary fought down a wave of panic. She hadn't the least idea how to help someone in this situation.

'Shall I phone for an ambulance?' she asked, hoping Dianne wouldn't notice the tremor in her voice.

'Yes. Ring the cottage hospital,' Dianne said, breathing deeply. She had been through childbirth twice before, so she was alternately groaning in pain, and then showing she was well prepared. 'And would you get my bag out of the wardrobe? I've packed everything I need.'

Galloping downstairs, Rosemary picked up the phone only to drop it again in her haste.

'Steady, girl,' she told herself, and gripped the receiver firmly.

A little later she helped Dianne downstairs and left her seated by the front door, then trotted back up to collect her bag. She was thinking that the best way to help at this time was to reassure the other woman that everything would be taken care of in her absence.

Panic gripped her for a moment as she thought of the responsibility she was taking on, but then she reminded herself that she'd held a responsible job in the WRNS. She could do this.

'Now, don't you worry about the children,' she said, summoning up a confident smile. 'I'll look after them.'

Dianne looked relieved. 'I was going to phone my mother to come over and collect them, but as Dad's none too well, I'd be ever so grateful if you'd be able to manage.'

Struck by Dianne's faith in her ability to become a nanny to three children after only two days' practice, Rosemary smiled and squeezed her friend's hand.

To help to pass the time until the

ambulance arrived, Rosemary found a notebook and jotted down Dianne's instructions, especially about the cooking.

After Dianne had been taken off to hospital, Rosemary rang Dianne's mother.

'Hello, Mrs Marshall. This is Rosemary Shepherd — '

'Oh, Rosemary. Dianne's been telling me what a wonderful person you are.'

Rosemary gulped. She wasn't used to being considered anything more than reasonably competent at her job.

'Dianne has just been taken into hospital, Mrs Marshall.'

'Is she all right?' She heard the concern in the woman's voice.

'Oh yes. But she's sure her baby is on the way . . . '

'Oh, dear. I said I'd have the children — '

'Don't worry, they can stay here with me.'

'Are you sure?'

Rosemary wasn't at all sure, but she didn't say so.

When she rang off she found she was

shaking. For goodness' sake, she told herself firmly, pull yourself together. You can weather this little storm.

She wandered into the kitchen.

'Now, what shall I do first?' she wondered aloud.

'Make me a cup of tea, if you will,' answered John Hythe, popping his head round the door. 'I did knock, but . . . '

Rosemary smiled, pleased to see him, and he stepped towards the range to warm his hands near the hot plate.

'Dianne's just been taken off to hospital,' she told him as she filled the kettle.

'I heard. I came as soon as I could,' he said. 'Sorry I missed her. But she's in good hands. I expect you're the one needing a little help.'

Grateful for his understanding of her situation, Rosemary smiled ruefully. 'I do feel a bit like a sinking ship,' she admitted and he laughed.

'Tell me all about it,' he said kindly as they sat down.

'You hear enough of other people's troubles . . . '

'Ah yes, but you're special.'

'A special case?' Rosemary felt her cheeks flame.

John shook his head. 'I didn't mean that. I meant you're special to me. And I'd like to help you — if I can.'

She was touched; he seemed genuinely concerned for her welfare.

'In that case, are you any good at putting up chicken wire?' she asked.

'Why?' He gave a chuckle. 'Are you going to enclose the Morton children in netting?'

'If only it was that easy,' she said, laughing.

'I don't suppose they'll be any trouble. They seem nice kids.'

'Oh, they are — and the Dutch boy, too. It's just that I'm not used to looking after children.'

He gave her hand a pat. 'They're old enough to look after themselves. All you have to do is keep an eye on them.'

'And feed them.'

'Well, yes. But they won't starve if you give them bread and marge for a few days.'

She laughed. 'I think even I can do a little better than that.'

'What do you want the netting for?'

Rosemary explained about Nicky and the chicken, and how Dulcie's little dog needed to be kept out of the chicken enclosure.

'I'm sure I can give you a hand with that,' he said, finishing his cup of tea. 'Come on, let's take a look.'

As they went outdoors, he said, 'I really came to tell you that my new car is being delivered next week, so you can have yours back.'

'Oh, that's fine,' said Rosemary, 'though I can't drive it without petrol.'

'We'll see about that. Did you find out who took the car the other day?'

'No. I've been too busy to even think about it. But it is a mystery.' As was her missing jewellery. And then there was all that black market stuff stored in the barn. She hadn't had time to cycle down to inform the police about everything. But she didn't want to burden John with that as well.

As they walked towards the hen house they found that the farmer had kindly brought along three more chickens, a big bag of cornmeal and a bale of straw, as well as a huge roll of chicken wire. Rosemary gulped when she saw it — the cost would be more than she had in the bank.

'Isn't that kind of Mr Hunt to bring us all this stuff?' she said. 'Aren't they lovely birds? With four hens we'll certainly have enough eggs for the family now.'

'You'll have to learn how to poach, scramble *and* fry them,' John said with a grin. 'Variety's the spice of life, remember.'

It wasn't an easy job removing the old chicken wire and fixing up the new stuff — and cold hands made it even more difficult. But Rosemary was impressed to see how handy John was.

'I thought you were a doctor in the

Navy, not a chippy,' she remarked.

'A carpenter has a lot of mending to do — and so has a doctor,' he said, seeming to enjoy the practical task.

It was after lunch-time when they'd finished, as Rosemary discovered when she glanced at her watch.

'Heavens!' she exclaimed. 'It's almost two o'clock.'

'Is it? I must dash to get to the surgery on time,' John said.

Concerned that he'd been working hard and had had nothing to eat, Rosemary felt guilty. But he assured her his housekeeper would feed him well in the evening.

★ ★ ★

Rosemary practised in her head what she was going to tell the children when they arrived back from school, hoping they wouldn't ask her too many awkward questions.

As it turned out, however, the Morton children had been well informed by their mother and took the course of events in their stride. Nicky, of course, was far more interested in the hens and went out to see them immediately.

'I hope Mum's baby is a boy,' said David. 'Then I can play with him.' And he galloped off to join Nicky.

'I hope it's a little sister for me. I'll give her my favourite doll,' said Susan. 'Do you know if the baby is going to be a boy or a girl?' she asked Rosemary.

Rosemary smiled. 'We should know before long,' she said. 'Now, I have to nip down to Mrs Richardson's and collect Hetty. Would you like to come with me?'

Susan nodded and they set off, Rosemary comfortably proud in the knowledge that she had already put some large baked potatoes in the oven, which they would have with some grated cheese and raw carrot for their supper when they got back.

Susan rode her fairy cycle, while Rosemary marched along the road to

Mrs Richardson's cottage at a brisk pace.

Dulcie was happy to see them, and talked to Susan while Rosemary did a few odd jobs. Then back they came to High Boughs.

After supper Rosemary made sure each child helped to clear the table and together they washed up. There was no grizzling; the children seemed to accept that they had to help now, and Nicky was clearly excited about his hens' accommodation.

'Will they lay us some eggs for breakfast?' asked Susan.

'You will have to look for them,' Nicky said.

Fascinated by the idea that there would be a treasure hunt for eggs, Susan and David jumped around the kitchen in excitement.

To quieten them down Rosemary suggested they listened to Children's Hour on the wireless and found one of her old jigsaw puzzles to keep them occupied until bedtime. She was thankful that she'd been able to keep them busy so that they didn't pine for their mother.

Rosemary herself lay awake late that evening, hoping for a phone call from the hospital to say Dianne's baby had been born. But no call came and she finally fell asleep.

★   ★   ★

Morning came with a splash of sunshine over the snow-covered fields and trees, which brightened everyone's mood.

Packing the children off to school, Rosemary promised them she would let them know if she heard any news about their mother.

It was with a sense of pride that she looked around her house later. The downstairs sitting-room hadn't been dusted for ages, so she did that, thinking it would be nice in the summer to be able to open the French windows and let the fresh air in. The dining-room had also been shut up and she longed to have the time to explore in there. She did notice the window in there was open a few inches and tutted. It was cold enough in the house without having draughts from open windows!

Going upstairs, she checked to see if the children had made their beds — which they had, after a fashion. She straightened out Susan's, though she hadn't done it badly for a five-year-old. The boys' beds were made but their room was a jumble of toys, books and clothes. She closed the door on it — she hadn't time to deal with it just now. She had to go and collect Hetty.

She checked the hens in passing, and found them pecking at the hard ground. Taking pity on them, she threw them another handful of corn.

Pedalling to Dulcie's cottage, she stopped at the farm gate and wondered how much she could afford to give the farmer. She had ten shillings, but she thought she might need that so she decided she'd have to wait till next week, when she would go to the post office and withdraw some more cash.

However, she did go in to thank him.

'Don't worry about paying me, m'dear,' he said kindly. 'You're looking after my hens and I would have to feed them anyhow. And I'm glad to help that Dutch lad. He seems to know more about poultry than I do! I could do with a young lad like that on the farm. My land girls are off soon and I don't know what I shall do then. I never thought those city girls would be any use when they came — but gracious me, they've certainly been hard workers. I shall miss them.'

Struck by his generosity, Rosemary thanked him profusely. At least one problem had been solved and she wouldn't be going to a debtor's jail.

Hetty had become accustomed to being collected every morning and waited patiently for Rosemary to arrive — and then what a racket she made as she ran around in circles and greeted her!

'Are you able to pop down to the village store? I need a few things. And do a little washing for me?' Dulcie asked.

Caught up by the household tasks, it was almost lunch-time when Rosemary arrived home, with Hetty in tow. Dulcie had persuaded her to take Hetty with her to save having to collect her later.

Rosemary decided she'd better have a quick bite to eat before tackling anything else. First thing she had to do in the afternoon was attempt to make pasties for supper, and some rock buns for the children, so she'd better get a move on. But as she went to fill the kettle, she froze — what was that noise?

It had come from somewhere inside the house.

Was there an intruder?

Then a door slammed upstairs and heavy footsteps headed downstairs.

Tip-toeing to the kitchen door, Rosemary opened it gingerly and peered out — and to her astonishment, she found herself face to face with an army officer. They stared at each other in confused silence for a moment.

At last he asked, 'Where's Mrs Morton?' rather sharply.

'She's in hospital, sir,' Rosemary said timidly.

He seemed taken aback. 'Is she unwell?' he asked.

'No, sir, she's having her baby.' Rosemary explained that she was expecting the phone to ring at any moment to say the child had been born.

'I'm Rosemary,' she added. 'And you are . . . ?'

He frowned as if he was trying to remember something. Then his face cleared.

'Of course, Miss Rosemary Shepherd — this is your house. My wife mentioned that you were coming home after doing your war service.'

The penny dropped. 'You're Captain Morton?'

'I am indeed.' They shook hands and as a smile replaced his anxious look,

Rosemary had the feeling she would like him.

'I'm on leave for a week,' he explained. 'I knew the baby was due around now and wanted to be with Dianne and the children. Who's looking after David and Susan?'

'I am.'

'Oh, that's very noble of you. Where are they just now?'

'At school. Sir, would you care to have a sandwich and a cup of tea before you set off for the hospital? I was just about to make something for myself.'

He gave a broad smile. 'I have to admit, that sounds most welcome. I've had quite a long journey.'

Over cups of tea they were soon on first name terms — his was Michael — as she put him in the picture about his family, then he was off again to the hospital, leaving his kit bag in the hall.

Rosemary managed to make some rather oddly-shaped Cornish pasties. They looked nothing like the beautifully-made traditional pasties with their neatly-twisted top, but they were the best she could do.

She chuckled as she popped them in the oven.

'They're not very pretty, but let's hope they taste all right.'

Unexpected Arrivals

More snow arrived that afternoon and as Rosemary watched large flakes floating by the kitchen window, she was pleased that she didn't have to collect the dog from Mrs Richardson. Hetty had come in from the garden as the snow began to fall and had settled comfortably in her box by the warm range.

Hoping the snow wouldn't become too deep before the children got home, she began some ironing, but she hadn't got far when the telephone rang.

It was Michael — a very excited Michael!

'Yes, Michael, I'll tell the children when they get home. They'll be delighted. Give my love to Dianne.'

'I will.'

Rosemary stood in the hall with a wide smile on her face. Fancy her feeling so radiantly happy about another family's birth.

'But,' she told herself, 'they're not another family. They're *my* family — at least, I can pretend they are!'

However, her euphoria drifted away later as the pile of ironing went steadily down and the kitchen clock ticked on and on — the children hadn't returned.

Hetty suddenly pricked up her ears and started barking. She ran to the front door as a key turned in the lock and a snowman came into the hall.

'Hello, Michael,' Rosemary called, coming out of the kitchen to join him. 'Don't mind the dog. Hetty's a yapper but she'll soon settle down.'

Mike squatted down and stroked the dog and Hetty soon stopped barking.

'There's a lot of snow coming down. I'm concerned about the children,' Rosemary remarked. 'It's four-thirty and they're not here yet!'

'Don't worry. I'll head down to the school and meet them,' Michael said.

Grateful to have someone to share

the responsibilities, she set about preparing the supper.

It wasn't long before cheerful voices were heard outside and Captain Morton returned with all three children. They came crowding in in a chattering, laughing group, setting Hetty off again, barking in delight.

'Hello, hello!' called Nicky. 'I'm starving!'

Rosemary looked at his wide grin and smiled. He was hungry, as usual, but he looked well-fed and healthy now — such a change from the poor waif he'd been when she'd first met him.

'The button has come off my coat,' said David, handing her a button. 'Can you sew it on for me, please?'

Rosemary chuckled; she must be managing well enough to be so easily accepted as their mother's substitute!

'Daddy says he has a secret to tell us,' said Susan with a hop, skip and a jump.

Michael winked at Rosemary. 'I told them I would tell them after supper,' he said.

Rosemary was pleased about that. She knew the children were excited to see their father home on leave, but they would be even more excited when he told them the news and she didn't want the little food they had to go to waste.

Michael looked tired. He'd travelled from up north to be with his family and had been on the cold, crowded train for hours. Rosemary's first thought was that she had to feed him and get him to bed — just like the children.

'All right, everyone — wash up and sit down,' she said in her Leading Wren voice.

The children scurried to do as they were told.

'You, too,' said Rosemary to Michael.

'Yes, ma'am,' he said with a grin.

As Rosemary put the pasties on the table, she grimaced.

'I'm sorry they look rather a mess. I can't make them like your mother, but I think they should taste all right.'

Nicky's mouth was already full.

'They are very good, Miss Shepherd,'

he assured her, and with this vote of confidence, they all tucked in.

Not a scrap was left and when the children had finished, they took the dishes to the sink.

Rosemary filled the sink with hot soapy water and David picked up the dish mop.

'Dad, watch me, I can wash the plates,' he said.

'And I dry them,' Nicky explained eagerly. 'I am tall and can put them in the plate rack.'

'I do the knives and forks,' Susan informed her father solemnly.

'My, Rosemary, you are indeed a wonder,' said Michael approvingly. 'The children have learned to lend a hand — what an achievement!'

She felt a warm glow of pride at his words.

'Did you remember to feed my hens?' Nicky asked Rosemary as he knelt to stroke the dog.

'They had plenty earlier on before it started to snow,' she told him.

She explained that she and Dr Hythe had put up the chicken wire and it would keep Hetty away from the hens.

'When you see Dr Hythe you should thank him, Nicky,' she added.

'Will your hens have chicks?' asked David.

'Talking about chicks,' interrupted their father, 'what about babies?'

David looked at him wide-eyed.

'Has Mum had her baby?'

The captain gave a wide smile and every face in the room lit up.

'She has, she has!' said Susan excitedly.

'Is it a boy?' asked David. 'I want a brother to play with after Nicky goes back to Holland.'

'I want a little sister,' said Susan. 'Please say I have a baby sister.'

'Well,' he said, frowning as he rubbed his chin in consternation. 'What are we going to do about that? David wants a boy and Susan wants a girl . . .'

The family waited so quietly for him to speak that they could hear the kitchen clock ticking.

At last he said, 'One boy, five and a half pounds . . . '

David shouted, 'Hurrah!'

' . . . and one girl, five pounds.'

The children looked puzzled.

'You said I had a brother,' David said indignantly.

'You have.'

'Is my sister a pretend sister?' Susan asked.

'She looked real enough to me when I saw her.'

'Twins!' said Nicky joyfully. 'Like a double-yolked egg!'

The noise level in the kitchen rose as everyone began to laugh and talk at the same time. What excitement!

It was after everyone had eventually settled down to have their bedtime cocoa and rock cakes that they started discussing the new babies' names.

'The names will have to wait until tomorrow. I'll be seeing Mum and we'll decide then,' Michael told them. 'But I will tell her your choices — although I think we can rule out some of your suggestions. I don't fancy a son called Rupert Bear, or a daughter called Goldilocks!'

After a good laugh, everyone went happily to bed.

★   ★   ★

That night, they all slept well. No-one awoke to hear Hetty barking in the kitchen, or her snuffling by the back door to be let out. She'd heard something going on at the bottom of the garden.

The 'something' was Horace Smith and his two grandsons, busy shifting some of the boxes from Rosemary's barn into a van.

'We'll never move all this lot tonight,' grumbled Alan Smith.

'I never said we would,' Horace said in a gruff voice. 'Now get on with it.'

'I'm tired,' said Brian, a weedy-looking young man. 'This lot's even heavier than it looks.'

'Let's nip down to the pub,' Alan suggested, looking at his watch. 'It ain't quite closing time.'

'Will you stop your moaning?' said their grandfather, heaving a box over to Alan. 'You two like having the money to buy your fancy suits and cars, don't you? You don't want to stand in a queue with your ration books to collect puny amounts of butter and cheese like everyone else, do you? And you want nylon stockings to give your girlfriends — as well as some warm wool coats and leather shoes to sell on the streets when the local bobby ain't looking.' He snarled louder, 'So, you need to do a bit of work for it, all right?'

'We've got enough cash for now, Grandad,' whined Brian. 'Can't we do this job tomorrow? The snow's slippery for carrying them boxes to the van.'

'Get a move on, I tell you,' Horace hissed. 'I think Miss Shepherd has got herself a dog. I can hear one barking in the house. And if she gets nosey and starts lookin' round her property, we could get caught. That'll mean prison for me, and Borstal for you two. And you lads wouldn't like that any more than I would. I've had enough spells in prison to last me a lifetime.'

Brian made a great fuss over taking one more box to the van. He came back shortly after, saying, 'The van won't take any more stuff.'

Horace swore under his breath. 'You're right. We'd better be off and come back tomorrow night.'

They clambered into the van and, Horace crunching the gears in his haste, they were soon trundling down the icy, rutted lane.

* * *

It was later next morning after the children had gone to school that Captain Morton told Rosemary that the housing officer had a house lined up for his enlarged family.

'But may we stay here for a little longer?'

126

'Of course!' said Rosemary, startled to realise how sorry she was to think of them all leaving. She had become very attached to them all.

Michael was clearly relieved and smiled at her.

'Thanks. The kids do seem settled with you. But I'll pay a woman to come in and help with the extra housework — and the babies.'

'Oh, you needn't do that,' she protested. '*I'm* the local home help.'

'Are you?' He looked pleased. 'Well, that's handy.'

'I'm no great shakes as a cook, though — but I'm learning.'

So that was settled. Rosemary gratefully received some crisp pound notes from Michael and thought that after the food shopping she had to do, the first thing she would buy for herself was a new pair of Wellington boots, because hers were beginning to leak after a good many years' service.

Michael went off to visit Dianne, leaving Rosemary wondering what she should do to accommodate two infants in the house. She decided to pop down to see Dulcie Richardson — she'd brought up a family and was sure to have some advice.

First of all, though, arrangements had to be made about the dog.

'Shall I bring Hetty over? And what jobs would you like me to do for you today?' she asked the woman.

'You're such a patient girl, Rosemary,' Dulcie said. 'Thank you for offering to help me this morning, but you'll have enough on your plate. I think I'll manage to do everything myself today without bothering you. And Hetty will get more exercise staying with the children — she's better off where she is.'

'I don't know about that. Hetty will be glad to get back to her peaceful home. The children are a little boisterous for her at times.'

Dulcie gave a little chuckle, and then gave Rosemary a lot of useful advice about babies.

Back home, Rosemary looked around and wondered where to start. Should she scrub the kitchen table and floor? Or clean the windows, or put the ironing away and do some more washing? Or make a shopping list and go down to the village store? And what on earth was she going to give the family for their supper?

Besides all that, she still hadn't found time to go to the police about the black market store in the barn!

It was as she stood pondering that she thought she heard a noise upstairs. She frowned. Had Michael returned without her noticing?

As she went upstairs, she was sure the noise she'd heard had come from her room, which definitely was puzzling. Hetty was outside in the garden chicken-watching, so who could it be?

She pushed open her bedroom door — and gasped in shock! The dark shape of a man was bending over her dressing table. A man she knew. She couldn't believe her eyes.

'Mr Clatterdove?' she gasped. 'What are you doing in my room?'

Taking a step nearer, she felt a surge of anger when she saw what Bill Clatterdove had in his hand. It was her jewellery box!

A Tricky Situation

Bill Clatterdove's head lowered and Rosemary noted his old eyes had tears in them, but seeing her pearl necklace falling half out of his macintosh pocket, she was too furious to feel sorry for him. She would never have thought in a million years that he could be the thief.

'I'd better explain,' Bill said in a broken voice.

'Yes, I think you had,' Rosemary agreed smartly.

Bill shifted his weight from one foot to the other.

'I know what you're thinking, Rosemary — '

'That you ought to be ashamed of yourself, Mr Clatterdove.'

'Indeed.' He nodded miserably. 'Forgive me. But please let me explain why I'm here.'

She felt a twinge of sympathy for the

old man when she saw his remorse. He had been her dad's best friend — and he had been kind to come and meet her at the station. So how did his thieving tie in?

She decided it would be better if they left the icy bedroom and went down into the warm kitchen.

'Come downstairs,' she suggested.

Her mind flitted to the other matter of the stolen goods in the barn. Did Bill Clatterdove have something to do with that as well?

'I wasn't — '

'Tell me in the kitchen,' she said, opening the door wide so that he could go out of the room first.

Glancing back, she was surprised to catch a glimpse of what looked like her charm bracelet on her dressing table . . .

Once in the kitchen, Bill sank onto a chair, bent forward and clasped his hands together as he stared at the floor. he looked utterly dejected.

'You were saying . . . you said you

can explain,' Rosemary prompted.

'It's Jimmy,' he said in a low voice.

'Who's Jimmy?'

Bill gave a sigh as he sat up.

'Jimmy Clatterdove is my grandson. My son was a medical man — killed at Dunkirk — and young Jimmy has become a right tearaway.'

He looked at the floor again and shook his head.

'He's been staying with me this last month or so because his mother says he's out of hand and she wants me to try to get him back on the right road. He's a young fool, Rosemary — he thinks stealing is a game.'

'So,' she said, as the truth dawned on her, 'it was Jimmy who took my jewels?'

'I'm afraid so. When I saw them in his room, I gave him what for, I can tell you. I was trying to put them back in your jewel box.'

Rosemary felt tears in her eyes. To think she had been accusing this gentle old man of theft when all he was doing was trying to repair the harm his grandson had done to her!

'Oh, Mr Clatterdove, I am so sorry,' she murmured. 'I thought — I thought that — '

He waved away her apologies. 'It was only natural you should think it was me who had stolen the jewels when you saw me standing there — I don't blame you.'

They looked into each other's eyes and smiled a little.

'Let's have a cup of tea,' Rosemary offered gently, 'and you can tell me all about this problem with Jimmy.'

'He's fifteen,' Bill told her. 'He left school last year and with nothing to do he's up to all kinds of mischief. He drove off in your car the other evening and I had to take it back to your garage.'

Ah! That explained that mystery. And not only had she left the keys in the car, she also remembered seeing that open dining-room window; it would have been only too easy for a burglar to enter the house.

'I'm terrified the police will be on to him soon and send him away,' Bill went on, his voice breaking. 'It would break my Godfrey's heart, God rest his soul, if he could see Jimmy behaving like this. And really, he's not a wicked lad — he's just thoughtless of how much his high spirits harm others. I wish he could find a job that would give him something worthwhile to do.'

'Hmm,' said Rosemary, thinking. 'I might be able to help you there,' she said, and a look of hope lit up the old man's face. 'I can't tell you anything yet, but I'll let you know,' she promised. 'Now, is that my pearl necklace hanging out of your mac pocket?'

Bill drew it out and put it gently on the table.

'I think we should go upstairs again and let you check that I've returned everything,' he said.

So they did — and, of course, everything was there.

★ ★ ★

When Bill had gone, Rosemary realised the whole morning had gone by and she'd done none of the jobs she'd hoped to do. But, looking through her returned jewellery once more, she decided that there was nothing more important at the moment than trying to do something to help Bill with his problem of young Jimmy. It sounded as if the lad was going off the rails fast, and Bill really was too old to cope with the responsibility.

She put Hetty on her lead. 'Come on, Hetty — time for a walk.'

As she stepped outside, the sun came out, filling Rosemary with hope about her plan.

Arriving at the farm, she found Mr Hunt feeding his pigs.

'You have a lot of work to do, Mr Hunt,' she observed.

'I do that — I wish I could find someone who likes animals to help.'

'How about a strong lad who needs to be worked to death?'

That caught his interest, and she

explained about Jimmy.

'You'll have to keep a strict eye on him, Mr Hunt. He needs keeping in order.'

'I was a bit of a handful myself at that age, Miss Shepherd,' Mr Hunt replied. 'And I won't give him time to get into mischief. Tell Mr Clatterdove to send him along at four tomorrow morning.'

'Did you say *four*? In the *morning*?'

'That's the time the cows are milked,' he replied with a grin.

'Well, I can't promise you he'll be here on the dot,' Rosemary said with a laugh, 'but I'll certainly pass on the message.'

Mr Hunt nodded. 'Fine. Just before you go, Miss — my wife's just cured some hams and has some end cuts which she can give you for all them kids you're feeding.'

Rosemary was delighted and left ten minutes later armed with a ham knuckle — what a treat for the children's tea!

★　★　★

It was a happy evening when Captain Morton returned to report that his wife and the new babies were thriving. Then they went on to discuss the babies' names.

'We wondered about calling the boy Charles, after his grandfather,' Michael said.

'Charles?' David repeated scornfully. 'That's a stuffy name!'

'No, it's not!' cried Susan. 'I like it.'

'And we thought of calling the girl Sonia, after your grandmother,' their father continued.

'I like that name,' said Nicky.

'I don't,' said Susan.

There followed a chorus of suggestions for names followed by howls of laughter as the children came up with ever more silly ideas.

Rosemary was glad that Michael was entertaining them. It gave her the chance to check the larder and the cupboards to see what she needed to buy when she went shopping in the morning.

She was adding another item to her shopping list when she heard the family calling for her attention.

'What do you think?' they all said together.

'I'm sorry — I wasn't paying attention,' said Rosemary, vaguely, thinking she should be making the evening cocoa now.

'Come here and we'll tell you.' Susan came to take Rosemary's hand, drawing her towards everyone.

'You tell her, Dad,' said David.

Michael cleared his throat. 'My wife and I decided to ask you,' he said and Rosemary's jaw dropped open in astonishment. What had naming their children to do with her?

'Oh, I don't think I should decide . . .' she began.

The children laughed and she looked round in bewilderment. What was the joke?

'No, no,' said Michael, seeing she was confused. 'I meant — we wondered if you would mind if we named our little girl Rosemary? Only she would be called Rose, so as not to muddle her name with yours.'

'Oh!' Rosemary blinked back sudden tears of joy. 'Of course I don't mind — it's an honour.'

Michael smiled. 'Thank you. You and Nicky have been part of our family for only a short time, but my wife and I don't want you forgotten when we all split up. So we decided to ask the two of you if we could call our babies Rosemary or Rose, after you, and the boy Nicholas, after Nicky.'

What a wonderful idea! Nicky obviously thought so too — his chest was swollen with pride.

Rosemary turned away quickly as fresh tears formed.

'I'd — I'd better make your cocoa,' she said with a sniff.

Her joy had evaporated at Michael's words. She wasn't crying about the little girl being called after her — of course she was pleased about that; she was crying at the thought of the family going away and leaving her. Alone.

★ ★ ★

It was after nine that evening, while Michael was reading the newspaper and Rosemary was sewing the button on David's coat, that there was a rap on the kitchen door and in came John Hythe.

'Evening, all!' he greeted them with a big smile.

On seeing him, a wave of happiness spread through Rosemary, which she immediately scolded herself for.

'I've come to return your car,' John said, giving her a light kiss on her cheek as he handed her the car key. 'Thanks for the use of it. It's in good order and the tank's full of petrol.'

'That's very kind of you,' she said, flushing as she looked into his merry eyes, while thinking it would be a great help tomorrow with all the shopping she needed for the family.

'No, indeed — it was good of you to lend it to me.'

Embarrassed, Rosemary asked him

about his new car.

'It's big and black — smells new,' he said, smiling. 'I'm very pleased with it.'

The two men were soon engaged in conversation about motors and Rosemary left them to it while she went to make the doctor some cocoa.

'By the way, Rosemary,' said John as she brought him a steaming cup, 'did you go to the police about that stuff in the barn?'

She coloured. 'No, I'm afraid I didn't. I was rather hoping they'd simply move it somewhere else. In any case, I haven't had the time.'

'Well, as I was driving the car towards the garage,' said John, 'I met a van coming along the lane and I'd swear it came from your barn. Anyway, when I'd put the car in the garage, I went along to the barn to take a look myself. There was no one there — but there were footprints in the snow which were too big to be the children's.'

Michael was plainly curious as to

what John was talking about, so they told him all about the black-marketeers.

'They've obviously been using my barn to store stuff for some time. They'd built up an enormous amount of it,' Rosemary said. 'The last time I looked there were masses of boxes there. Now I suppose they're taking it away in this van you've seen and it's taking them a long time to shift it.'

'Something ought to be done to catch them,' said John. 'I've seen people in dire need of food and clothing this winter — it's not right that rations are being stolen and sold on for the profit of a few mean crooks.'

'Quite right,' said Captain Morton. 'Well, I'm here for a few days. Let's plan an attack and we'll put an end to their caper.'

Rosemary felt anxious — and a twinge of guilt gnawed at her. She knew she should have gone to the police long ago. But she'd kept putting it off. Oh, not intentionally, but she realised now that she should have phoned them right away and got the whole situation sorted out.

Still, there was nothing to be gained by fretting now over what should have been done, she decided. And there was one thing to be thankful for — her stolen jewels had been returned and she didn't have to report them missing at the same time.

'Will you be going to the police?' she asked Michael.

'I certainly shall,' he said. 'But there's only one village policeman and he can't be expected to stay out in the perishing cold to collar those villains all on his own. We'll have to help.'

After a little more discussion, John reluctantly stood up and prepared to leave. He shook hands with Michael, and congratulated him on the birth of the twins. Then he gave Rosemary another swift kiss on the cheek, wrapped his scarf tightly around his neck, put on his hat, and limped out of the door.

'Take care, John,' Rosemary called

after him and he turned and waved to her.

'He seems to like you, Rosemary,' Michael commented, observing her closely and noticing the high colour of her cheeks.

She gave a dismissive laugh. 'John's known me since we were as young as your children are,' she said, trying to keep her voice light. 'We're old pals.'

'That may be so, but if you ask me, he thinks of you as more than a friend,' he commented with a grin.

Rosemary had to think quickly to hide her embarrassment.

'A doctor has to be able to get on with people,' she said briskly, collecting the dirty cups and taking them to the sink to wash.

'Yes, but I bet he doesn't give everyone a peck on the cheek like that,' Michael remarked. 'He seems a nice bloke, Rosemary. It would be nice if you two . . .

'Michael!' Her voice was sharp as she interrupted him. 'You should know that

Dr Hythe is a married man.'

'Oh.' Michael picked up the dish towel and said no more.

But the damage had been done. It took a long time for Rosemary to fall asleep that night. The image of John persisted in invading her thoughts.

Married or not, she couldn't deny she liked him very much.

Operation Catchem

Several days later, Michael was able to tell the children that their mother was bringing their new brother and sister home the next day. The children capered about with excitement and Rosemary had trouble calming them down enough to sit down for their supper.

'Now listen,' he said before the meal was put on the table, 'I'm afraid there's bad news too. My leave is almost over. I have to go back to camp tomorrow.'

A chorus of disappointed 'Ahs!' came from the children.

Michael smiled. 'I'll miss you too. But I hope to hear we have married quarters ready for us very soon and you and Mum will come and join me.'

Rosemary, who was at the range mashing some potatoes to go with the sausages, smiled a little sadly, knowing how much she would miss them all.

'In the meantime,' Michael went on, 'your mother and Rosemary are going to be very busy looking after the twins. Rose and Nicholas will need feeding and bathing, so I hope you're going to keep on helping them as much as you can. You've been so good up till now.'

Three eager faces showed that they were willing.

'Good. And no slacking, mind, or I'll hear all about it!' he added with a wink at Rosemary.

'I suppose I ought to take Hetty back to Dulcie this evening, with the babies arriving,' Rosemary murmured. There was going to be a lot of extra noise in the house once Dianne and the babies came home, so the old dog would probably prefer being quiet with her mistress again.

Rosemary was in two minds about it herself. She wasn't used to babies. She couldn't say she was overjoyed at the prospect of nappies drying around the kitchen either, but the weather was too cold for them to dry outside. There was nothing else for it — they would all have to get on with things as usual.

After supper she rang Dulcie Richardson and asked her about taking Hetty back.

'Well, the weather isn't quite so bitter — at last!' said Dulcie. 'I'm able to get about more easily, so I can let Hetty out in the garden whenever she wants to go. You'll have your hands full with two babies in the house, so I can understand you won't want Hetty under your feet.'

Rosemary didn't feel quite so sure about that. She loved the old dog as much as Dulcie, and deep down she really wanted Hetty to stay.

She was beginning to realise just how lonely she would be after the family left. For the present, however, Dulcie was right: she was going to be very busy once the babies arrived and since she'd given the dog to Dulcie, she couldn't go back on that. If the old lady wanted her to be returned to her cottage, then back she would have to go.

Dulcie was still talking. 'I've been thinking, Rosemary — although I love your visits and the way you help me, it might be better if I try to manage without your help until the Morton family leave. You'll have enough to do with the five kiddies.'

Rosemary was pleased that Dulcie felt well enough to manage on her own, but she felt even happier when Dulcie told her that she wanted her to come back to work for her after the family left. It meant she would still see Hetty occasionally — and she'd still have her job!

She arranged to deliver the dog to Dulcie in the morning and then said goodbye.

Michael was waiting for her to finish her phone call. He beckoned her into the sitting room where they could talk privately.

'The kids are playing Snakes And Ladders, but I'll get them off to bed soon.' His voice lowered. 'Tonight I plan to catch the black-marketeers.'

A little shiver went down Rosemary's spine.

'I've been down to the barn and reckon tonight might be our last chance before everything has been moved,' he told her quietly.

'What's your plan?'

'We'll hide until the thieves arrive, then surprise them.'

'What if they run away?'

Michael grinned. 'They're bound to try to run, aren't they? But don't worry — I've called it 'Operation Catchem' — and that's what I intend to do.'

Rosemary was unconvinced.

'How many men do you reckon there are to catch? You might be able to tackle one, but I can't.'

'The village policeman's going to watch for the van coming to the barn tonight, and he'll be there to help.'

'But say there are three of them?' Rosemary was beginning to panic, although Michael sounded very calm about it all.

'Ah, that's where you come in.'

'Me?' she gasped. 'What good do you think I'll be?'

'You'll be hidden with a torch to give the impression that there are more police about, so that the crooks will give themselves up.'

Michael's grin was broad and confident but Rosemary's heart sank. She couldn't help thinking that there were all sorts of things that could go wrong with 'Operation Catchem'.

Unfortunately, though, she couldn't think of anything better.

★   ★   ★

The garden was eerie in the moonlight.

It wasn't as cold as it had been, but the ground was still as hard as rock and the bare branches of the trees looked like begging hands reaching up to the sky pleading for heat from the pale moon.

Rosemary, crouched behind the hen-house and a laurel bush, shivered. She was well hidden by the evergreen leaves but she still felt vulnerable.

The torch in her gloved hand was ready to switch on when she received the signal from Michael. All she'd been asked to do was to put on her torchlight and move about.

Would those black-marketeers never come? She seemed to have been waiting there in the cold, damp grass for hours. Her Wellingtons were letting in the wet. She stamped her feet to try to warm her toes but all she heard was a squelchy sound, and her feet remained like blocks of ice.

An owl hooting made her jump.

She and Michael had made sure the children were safely tucked up in bed, and the dog was curled up in her box, before they'd crept out of the back door. But she'd seen Hetty opening one eye and noting their furtive exit.

After what seemed like hours, she spotted the twin beams of a vehicle's headlights coming along the lane. The sound of a motor engine became louder, and then a van swung on to the concrete drive by the garage.

The van's lights snapped off, but torchlights were visible and men's muffled voices could be heard as the van door opened.

At last! Now it was just a case of netting the villains.

For a while she heard nothing more, but straining her eyes to see, she could just make out some men carrying boxes towards the van. This went on for a few minutes and she wondered when Michael would strike.

'Right, that's the lot,' she heard a man's voice say eventually.

'Let's push off then. I want a pint before closing time,' said another.

Wasn't Michael going to make a move?

'The van's not full,' said yet another voice. There were three of them then? 'Let's have a scout around and see what else might be useful.'

Rosemary's eyes widened at their greed. And then fear gripped her as she heard them moving around the garden.

Next moment, she spotted two youths coming her way. What would they do to her if they discovered her? Where was Michael, for heaven's sake?

'Wow, just look at them hens,' exclaimed one of the youths. He had opened the hen-house door and disturbed the fowl, who started clucking loudly.

'Let's take them birds. We could sell them.'

It was all too much for Rosemary. How dare they! Well, she certainly wasn't about to stand there and do nothing to prevent it.

'Oh, no, you don't!' Her Leading Wren voice rang loud and clear all over the garden.

The chickens were beginning to protest wildly, too, at having their night's sleep disturbed. They ran out of the hen-house, squawking and sending feathers flying through the air.

The men flashed their torchlights in Rosemary's face. Blinded, she screamed.

The hens squawked like sirens as

they flew out of their enclosure and ran around the garden.

'Quick! Someone's going to hear the racket them hens are making. Make a run for it!' she heard one lad call to the other.

A wave of relief swept over her as she realised they were leaving, but it was soon overtaken by anger as it occurred to her that it meant they would escape without punishment after all . . .

All of a sudden, to Rosemary's surprise, they seemed to be seized by panic, pelting for their van, yelling, 'Start the van! There's a whole load of them!'

Rosemary couldn't understand why they thought she was any more than one scared female, until she noticed a shaft of light had suddenly shone from the kitchen and a dog streaked out, barking loudly and snapping at the intruders' heels. A stream of pyjama-clad figures raced after the dog, screaming like banshees.

'Hetty, help me round up my hens!'

Fleet of foot, Nicky was yelling as he raced after the dog, anxious to know why his hens had got loose.

It was a chaotic and noisy scene. Rosemary stood gasping for breath as a confused jumble of voices and lights darted around the garden like fairy spirits.

The two younger men were running back towards the van when Michael suddenly leaped out and felled one of them with a competent rugby tackle.

The older man, who had started the van when he heard the commotion, tried to turn the vehicle quickly to make a getaway, but he found his exit blocked by a police car.

Rosemary rushed after the third man, but he was a young lad who sprinted faster than she could. He made a mistake, however, when he raced into the barn to hide. Rosemary hared after him and promptly slammed the doors closed behind him, then used the wooden bar to lock him in.

But her ordeal hadn't finished.

Nicky suddenly appeared and handed her one of his hens.

'Hold Wilhelmina for me,' he said breathlessly as he darted off.

'And here's Lysbeth,' he said moments later. Rosemary struggled to hold another flustered hen.

Then she spied David, in his pyjamas, having a game chasing around the laurel bush, trying to catch another hen, Hetty barking at his heels.

After the tension of the evening, reaction set in and Rosemary could do nothing but sink to the ground, clutching the hens, tears of laughter rolling down her cheeks.

An Accident

Next morning, with so much to think about after last night's hazardous adventure, and so much to do with Dianne and the twins coming home that afternoon, Rosemary felt tired and headachy.

She was relieved that Nicky had seen to his birds while she helped the other children get ready for school. It was such a blessing that he was a responsible boy. Every morning, however cold, the Dutch boy went out into the garden to let them out of the hen-house into their run. And he fed them and made sure their water was de-iced. It was good for the two younger children to see and learn how animals had to be cared for, too, she thought.

'Another button's come off my coat,' David wailed, holding the button out for Rosemary to sew on.

'It's because you pull at the buttons instead of undoing them as you take your coat off,' she scolded.

'No, I don't,' David protested.

'Yes, you do,' Susan piped up, and her brother scowled at her.

Seeing a quarrel developing, and remembering that young David had been chasing a hen around the garden at midnight and was probably as tired as she was, Rosemary smiled at the sullen boy.

'Give it to me,' she said gently, taking the button. 'I'll sew it on for you.'

'What time is Mum coming home?' asked David, cheering up, as he watched Rosemary's needle busy at work.

'I'm not sure.'

'What's for tea?' asked Nicky.

'Wait and see,' said Rosemary, bundling them out of the door. 'Now, off you go — don't be late for school.'

Michael wanted a big breakfast. He would pack his bag ready to take the long train journey back to camp that evening, once he'd collected his wife and the babies from the hospital.

'I'm sorry to be leaving you with so many children to look after,' he said with an apologetic grin. 'I'll do all I can to hurry along the move to our new home.'

'Heavens,' said Rosemary, 'don't you worry about that — I enjoy having your family here.'

'You'll have it all at your fingertips when you have your own family, won't you?' he said and Rosemary nearly choked on her toast. Not for one moment could she envisage having a family of her own. Not now Rob had gone . . . and John . . .

Then they discussed the previous night's adventure: Operation Catchem.

'I'll have to go to the police station first thing this morning and give a statement,' Michael said.

'Do the police know anything about the men we caught?'

'I understand it was an old man, Horace Smith, who was in charge of the black market operation. He'll probably be found guilty because he has quite a criminal record. The others were his grandsons. They'll most likely be sent to Borstal, where I hope they'll learn to mend their ways.

'The war has caused such a lot of upheaval for many families,' he mused. 'Young men are often at a loose end and get up to mischief.'

Rosemary nodded, reflecting how glad she was that she hadn't reported young Jimmy Clatterdove to the police.

'Oh, well, I've a busy day ahead of me,' she said briskly, starting to collect the dishes together to be washed, 'so I'd better get started.'

'Me too,' said Michael. 'Thanks for the lovely breakfast. Now I must go and pack my kit.'

Rosemary was glad he hadn't noticed that there hadn't been enough bacon and eggs for two people; he'd presumed she'd already had her breakfast with the children.

But she was far from feeling sorry for

herself. She was excited about the day ahead and dying to see the twins.

* ★ ★

The awful winter was showing signs of ending at last. Blizzards and grey skies were replaced with a milder wind, and a bright blue sky made the icicles hanging on tree branches sparkle and drip in the weak sunshine.

It was bright and sunny when Rosemary clipped on Hetty's lead and set off for Dulcie's cottage, enjoying the picturesque scenes of the snowy fields and hedges.

Before leaving, she had hurriedly prepared a hot-pot for tea and checked that the children had made their beds before they went off to school. She also put an electric fire in Dianne's room ready to switch on and take the chill off the air.

She hoped the fresh air would clear her head as she strode along the lane.

Although sad to be saying goodbye to

the little dog, she felt Dulcie and Hetty were made for each other. Just as it was right for the Mortons to live together at Michael's camp's married quarters, she mused — and young Nicky should go back to his own family and homeland.

'I should like to have my own family,' she told Hetty suddenly and her heart was heavy at the realisation. For how could that ever happen? Rob was gone . . . and soon everyone else would be gone, too. She would be alone.

★ ★ ★

Rosemary hadn't been home for more than five minutes when the telephone rang.

' . . . ello? It's 'ill,' she heard as she picked up the phone.

Rosemary frowned. Who on earth — ?

'Who is this?' she asked.

''Ill . . . Dove,' the voice repeated.

Was this some kind of a joke? Then it dawned on her. Bill Clatterdove!

'Oh, Bill, I'm sorry, I didn't hear you properly.'

He mumbled on and Rosemary soon realised he was in trouble. He'd lost his false teeth — and his spectacles, too, so he was unable to look for them.

'I'll come round to help you look for them,' she offered at once. With a sigh, she hoped to get there and back quickly. And to do that she would have to cycle.

Making a mental note to get her own bike repaired, she grabbed Dianne's and set off.

Bill was most grateful that she'd come round.

'It's my age,' he moaned. 'I keep forgetting where I put things.'

It wasn't his age at all, Rosemary thought — he was just plain untidy. His house was in a terrible mess.

'I'm not surprised you can't find anything, Bill. You've got everything everywhere,' she said somewhat bossily as she made a start on going through the rooms, looking for his missing belongings.

'My wife used to say that,' said Bill.

'You need a Mrs Mop to tidy up for you,' said Rosemary, lifting a heap of old newspapers which were piled on the floor near his fireside chair to see if his teeth had fallen under them.

'I do indeed,' said Bill.

The kitchen was a disgrace and Rosemary almost rolled up her sleeves to start cleaning it, but then she remembered she hadn't time right now.

After working her way systematically through the house, she finally found his glasses in the bathroom, and his teeth in the teapot!

They both laughed.

'I remember now, I was going to put my teeth in and make a cup of tea this morning . . . ' he murmured. 'I must have put my dentures into the pot instead of the tea.'

'Well, I'll stick the kettle on for you now, just before I go,' Rosemary offered, glad to have sorted out his problem.

As he watched her, Bill told her that

she had sorted out another problem for him, too, for young Jimmy had taken to farm work like a duck to water.

'He's having to work hard,' he said, 'but he's enjoying it. And he likes Mr Hunt and Mrs Hunt feeds him so it looks like I don't have to worry about him at all.'

Rosemary was pleased to hear that.

'And,' said Bill, 'his first month's wages are going towards paying for Nicky's hens and feed — so you don't have to worry about paying Mr Hunt for them.'

'Oh, Jimmy doesn't have to do that!' Rosemary protested.

'Yes, he does,' Bill insisted. 'He knows he did wrong to take your jewellery, and he agrees with me that the best way to show he's proper sorry is to do something to help you out.'

Rosemary smiled, realising that she would probably have done the same had their positions been reversed. And it meant she didn't have to worry about paying Mr Hunt for some time, which was certainly a relief.

'Please thank Jimmy,' she said, 'and when the Mortons are gone — which I understand will be very soon — I'll come and spring clean your house, Bill.'

Bill was very pleased to hear that Rosemary's job was house cleaning and he offered her a generous wage to come to do his a couple of mornings a week.

They shook hands on their agreement and then Rosemary had to hurry away, only pausing at the village shop to collect some fresh vegetables and a bottle of aspirin for her headache.

She needed a rest when she got back, but time was ticking by fast and she only had time for a quick sandwich before the Mortons arrived home.

★   ★   ★

They're adorable!' exclaimed Rosemary, looking at the two tiny faces and bodies wrapped up in their shawls. 'Which is which?'

'Here's Nicholas,' said Michael, indicating one child. 'He's slightly heavier than his sister.' He carefully handed the other baby to Rosemary. 'And this is Rose,' he said quietly.

A thrill went through Rosemary at being given her namesake to hold — a thrill that was half pleasure, half pain.

She kissed the child and then gave her back to Dianne who looked tired, but happy to be back in her bedroom with her babies.

Michael was happy too, but remembering that his leave was over and they had only a few hours together, Rosemary decided to leave them alone and excused herself to make some tea.

Brushing away a tear, she turned her mind to the practicalities of running the household. At least she had learned quite a lot about that over the past few weeks, whereas babies were still unknown territory.

Thankfully, there was some cooking to be done for tea and for the next hour she was busy getting things ready.

She must have dozed sitting in a chair by the warm range until there came a knocking at the front door.

Rosemary started. Who could it be? Whoever it was was very impatient, knocking persistently like that.

Stepping sleepily into the hall, she saw Michael coming downstairs and called, 'I'll see who it is.'

Outside were two women. One was muscular, her lace-up shoes planted firmly apart as she looked at Rosemary with a grim expression. The other was more slight and her hair drooped forward as she blinked at Rosemary through her spectacles.

'Hello,' said Rosemary, 'can I help you?'

The larger woman gave a snort. 'What you can do, Miss Shepherd — or what you should have done — is to look after the children in your care.'

Now it was Rosemary's turn to blink. The smile disappeared from her face as she looked at the unfriendly ladies. Before she could say anything, the loud woman informed her that the other woman was the policeman's wife.

'Hello,' said Rosemary weakly, wondering what this visit was all about.

She didn't have long to wonder. Wagging her finger in Rosemary's startled face, the overbearing woman began to tell her, in no uncertain terms, just exactly what it was about. The truth of the matter was that she, Miss Shepherd, had broken the law!

'And what's more, Miss Shepherd,' the woman continued sharply, 'I'll have you know that your carelessness has allowed a boy to nearly drown!'

'What are you talking about?' Rosemary gasped, alarmed.

'My name is Miss Fairclough. I'm a magistrate, and I should know what I'm talking about. The boy has been taken to hospital. But Mrs Whittington and I saw him first.' She turned to the other lady. 'Didn't we see him all pale with his teeth chattering? I said he won't last long.'

'W . . . which boy?' Rosemary stuttered.

'The children said he was from Holland — and that *you* are supposed to be looking after him!' Miss Fairclough puffed out her large bosom. 'Fine way to look after the child! He shouldn't have been allowed to skate on the pond. The ice cracked and he went straight through it!'

'You shouldn't have allowed him to skate,' agreed the constable's wife.

The larger lady raised her voice. 'He could have drowned all the other children down by the pond, too, the way he was encouraging them to skate as well!'

Rosemary's hand went to her face. Nicky! Had Nicky been hurt?

'You've acted in a very irresponsible manner, Miss Shepherd and I'd like to say . . .'

But Rosemary didn't want to hear what either of these women would like to say. She'd had enough of their overbearing attitude. They seemed more concerned with scolding her than with the tragedy of a life in peril.

As a Leading Wren during wartime, she had tackled some unpleasant situations and some equally unpleasant people. She looked the two harridans in the eyes and interrupted sternly.

'For your information, I did not give Nicky permission to skate. As far as I know he hasn't any skates. He's a responsible boy, but could have mistaken the thickness of the ice. They do a lot of skating in Holland and I dare say he might have been showing the other children how they skate in his homeland.'

Taken aback by her sudden show of authority, the two ladies took a step backwards as Rosemary went on.

'I presume, although you haven't had the courtesy to tell me, that our Dutch boy fell through the ice because he'd neglected to observe that a thaw has started and the ice is no longer thick enough for skating?' She glared at them. 'I can understand that Nicky would have suffered an unpleasant cold soaking — but since the village pond is probably not very deep, I doubt that he could have been in any danger of drowning in a few inches of water!'

Mrs Whittington, pushing a lock of her wayward hair nervously under her hat, appeared to agree.

'No, he couldn't really. He scrambled out.' Then, with a glance at her grim looking companion, she added, 'But he was very pale, wasn't he, Miss Fairclough?'

Rosemary didn't give Miss Fairclough a chance to say any more — she'd heard quite enough from them already.

'So, you're telling me that Nicky has been taken to hospital to recover from his icy dip, are you? Right then, I'll ring Dr Hythe and ask him about the boy. Now, what about the other children? They should be home by now — their parents are waiting for them with their new baby brother and sister.'

There was a silence.

'Captain Morton has to leave at six o'clock to take a train up north,' Rosemary said sharply. 'So where are his children?'

'I took them to my house,' said Miss Fairclough in a subdued tone.

Rosemary gave the busybody a withering smile. 'Then please bring David and Susan back here immediately.'

She was too furious to do more than close the front door with a clunk after the ladies had turned their backs on her.

But she felt shattered. Her head was pounding as she returned to the kitchen to find that the vegetable water had boiled over and was hissing on the hob. The hotpot should have been taken out of the oven and was being overcooked — and the cat tripped her up because it hadn't been fed.

Rosemary sank down on a kitchen chair and wept.

She had tried her best, she really had,

but it seemed as if all her efforts to be an efficient home help had failed. She had lost her temper with two village ladies and poor little Nicky had been taken to hospital! How ill he was she didn't know, but she was desperately worried about him.

A Sad Parting

Rosemary didn't hear Dr Hythe enter the kitchen and limp towards her. She only realised he was there when she felt a comforting arm around her shoulders and heard his deep voice in her ear.

'I'm sorry to see you unhappy, my dear. Can I help?'

Rosemary took out her hanky and dabbed at her tears.

'Two of the village women came and accused me of — of neglecting the children — ' she mumbled.

'Why?'

'They said it was my fault Nicky fell through the thin ice into the pond,' she said miserably. 'And . . . they said I was . . . ' She stopped as her tears flowed again.

'Take no notice of them. Boys will be boys. Nicky thought the ice was thicker than it was. I came to tell you he'll be fine.'

Rosemary looked at him through watery eyes. 'He's not badly hurt, then?'

'No, most certainly not. He'll likely catch a nasty cold after his icy dip, that's all. He told me he was up at midnight chasing hens and burglars, so he's very tired — and I dare say you are too.'

'Yes, I am,' she agreed wearily, 'and I've got a headache. And the supper's overcooked and I'm expecting the children back at any moment and they'll be hungry. And Mr and Mrs Morton are upstairs with their newborns . . .'

John looked sympathetically at her. 'You've a lot to cope with.'

'It has been very busy these last few days — ' she said as she blew her nose.

'And a night-time adventure! Tell me about it while I make you a cup of tea.'

He was good at listening, so Rosemary went on to tell him how she'd been upset at the thought of the Morton family leaving, and Nicky returning to Holland, and even Hetty having to be given back to Dulcie.

'I'll soon be alone here,' she explained, 'and I confess I was feeling sorry for myself,' she said.

'Understandable,' murmured John, placing a cup of tea in front of her.

Her fighting spirit returned as she took a sip of the warm liquid.

'I could have done without those two busy-bodies coming and wagging their fingers at me and blaming me for not looking after the children properly,' she said grimly.

'They don't know what they're talking about!' he insisted. 'You're doing a marvellous job of looking after them.'

Rosemary put her elbow on the table and propped her head in her hand, looking glum.

'They'll be in at any moment, and I've ruined their supper.'

'It might not be as bad as you think.'

He sniffed the air. 'There's a delicious smell coming from the oven.'

Rosemary got up and picked up the ovencloth to take out the hotpot.

'Look at it. It's burnt!' she cried, although she had to agree that it did smell good.

John came and looked over her shoulder.

'Well, maybe the potatoes are a darker brown than usual, but they look crispy and delicious to me. I'm sure it'll be fine for three hungry children.'

A wave of relief washed over her. He was right — the food wasn't quite the disaster she'd expected to see.

'Thank goodness!' she breathed. 'I was thinking I was a complete failure.'

'You? A failure? Not at all. You've worked wonders ever since you came home,' he said, patting her arm. 'The Mortons sing your praises, Mrs Richardson can't thank you enough, and Mr Clatterdove can see once more because you found his glasses — '

'And his teeth!' said Rosemary with a

chortle. She was feeling better now that she'd had a chat about her woes, and the aspirin she had taken with her tea had helped too.

They were still smiling at each other as the door crashed open and David came in at a run.

'Where's my new brother?' he demanded, excitedly.

'Steady on. You must go quietly,' Rosemary said. 'He's upstairs, with your mum and dad.'

'Hello, Dr Hythe,' David said as he struggled out of his coat. 'Is Nicky OK?'

'Yes, he is. He's being kept in hospital overnight because Rosemary has enough to do looking after the Morton family.'

'Oh, she can manage us,' said David airily. 'Wow! Tea smells super.'

'It's a little overcooked,' admitted Rosemary.

'Who cares? I'm famished — and since Nicky's in hospital, I'll be able to have a second helping, won't I?'

Rosemary had to giggle as he ran

upstairs, calling back over the banisters, 'I hope you've made some more rock cakes.'

'You see, the children are happy enough with what you do — and that's what matters,' said John. 'Those two women were just whipping up trouble that doesn't exist. Forget about them and let's get the supper ready for everyone.'

Moments later, Susan came in, panting.

'A horrid bossy woman kept me at her house after Nicky fell in the pond,' she said. 'I kept saying I wanted to come home to see my baby sister, but she wouldn't listen.'

Rosemary soothed the little girl as she helped her to take off her coat, hat and mittens. Soon Susan was scampering upstairs to join her family, delighted at the prospect of a new little playmate to share her dolls with.

'Well, I'd better take a meal up to Dianne,' said Rosemary. 'I'll give them a few minutes and then call Michael and the children to come down here to eat.'

'Good idea.'

John found a tray and began to dish up a plateful for Dianne.

'You don't have to stay and help,' Rosemary protested, taking some knives and forks from the drawer.

'I'd like to, if you don't mind,' John replied. 'I like being with you.' And to her surprise, he gave her a rather bashful grin. She hoped he didn't notice her blush.

He was being kind and helpful, and after her run-in with the village busybody and her worry over Nicky, she really appreciated his company. It was nice to have someone taking a share of the workload, too.

It was such a shame he was married, a small voice whispered in her mind.

She felt a pain in her heart. She wasn't proud of herself, but she had become aware she had fallen in love with this kind man. She'd done her best to ignore the feelings, but when it came down to it, there really wasn't anything she could do about it — except, of course, keep her unrequited love buried deep inside and never mention it to anyone.

Fortunately, she didn't have much time to think about it because Michael came down with David and Susan soon afterwards, all looking forward to supper.

The hotpot wasn't nearly as bad as Rosemary had feared and the extra-crunchy potatoes went down well. John, who stayed to join them, smiled at her with a twinkle in his eye as every plate was cleared.

After supper, Michael had to say goodbye and leave his family.

Then it was time to put the excited children to bed, and Dianne and the babies needed attention too. But John was a great help and his calm manner did much to soothe her nervousness at holding the tiny newcomers.

Once everyone was settled, John fetched his hat and coat.

'Now, an extra cup of cocoa for you tonight and then get yourself off to bed,' he said. 'Doctor's orders, all right? You're going to need all your energy over the next few days.'

Remembering his kind, twinkling eyes, Rosemary was sure she wouldn't be able to sleep, but exhaustion took over and she drifted off as soon as her head touched her pillow.

★ ★ ★

Molly Perkins, the district nurse, came tripping in early the next morning.

'I didn't know you were coming,' said Rosemary, surprised, 'but I'm very glad to see you — I've no experience of looking after babies.'

'Dr Hythe asked me to put Mrs Morton on my list. He told me you were pressed with so much to do,' Molly explained with a warm smile. 'I'll pop in whenever I can.'

Taking Molly upstairs, Rosemary began to learn about caring for the

185

babies from a real expert.

'Mrs Morton is a very sensible mother,' Molly said before leaving. 'She'll be able to move around more in a day or so and cope with the babies on her own. I'll be back to see you this evening.'

Rosemary couldn't thank her enough for coming. Then, having waved the nurse goodbye, she started on the daily chores.

She was surprised when Nicky came in, with a wide smile — and a sneeze.

'Oh, Nicky, I'm so pleased to see you. Are you feeling all right? You were unlucky to fall through the ice.'

The Dutch boy continued to beam at her and Rosemary stepped forward to give him a hug and a kiss.

'Don't!' he cried, stepping back from her.

With a pang, Rosemary realised that boys of his age didn't like being kissed — and besides, he didn't want her to catch his cold.

But she was wrong about the reason

for his reluctance to let her near him. He suddenly produced an egg from his pocket.

'There,' he said proudly, holding it out to her. 'You see, I didn't want you to squash it!'

She watched in amazement as he produced another egg — and another!

'Heavens,' she exclaimed. 'You're like a magician. How many more?'

With a flourish Nicky found the last egg and laid it carefully on the table. Five beautiful oval-shaped brown eggs gleamed in front of her. Afraid they might roll off the table, she grabbed a bowl from the dresser to put them in.

'Freshly-laid eggs for tea. That's going to be a wonderful treat!' She put her arm around him and kissed him on the cheek. 'Well done, Nicky. Thank you. Now, I expect you'll want to go and see the new babies?'

He sneezed several times by way of reply.

'Oh dear me! You're getting a nasty cold after your dip in the pond.'

Nicky nodded. 'Dr Hythe says I must be careful not to breathe on the babies. I'll keep my handkerchief over my face and peep over it to see them — see?'

Rosemary smiled at his eyes twinkling over the handkerchief.

★ ★ ★

Unfortunately, over the next few days Nicky's cold spread to Rosemary, David and Susan. Fortunately, by keeping the children out of Dianne's room, mother and babies were not infected.

Molly praised Rosemary.

'You did very well to keep the children away from their mother. Fortunately the twins are very good babies — they're not giving Mrs Morton any trouble at all. She's lucky — although I know you've helped her a lot. She says you've been a treasure.'

Rosemary felt flattered.

'It's been fun for me to get out my

old board games to play with the children. Ludo and Snap, and listening to Toy Town and the Ovaltineys on the radio made me feel like a girl again.'

'You *are* still a girl!'

'Oh, Molly, I'm twenty-two! An ex-service woman — I feel like an old maid.'

'No, you're not.' Molly chuckled. 'You're full of go and ready to make someone an excellent wife.'

Rosemary grimaced. 'There aren't many prospective husbands in this village.'

'Well, I can think of one at least,' said the nurse, clipping her leather bag shut.

'Oh? Who?'

'Dr Hythe, of course.' Molly laughed. 'Surely you've noticed him?'

'Well, yes. He's been a good friend to me. But — he's married.'

The nurse shook her head. 'He *was* married.'

Rosemary's mouth went dry. 'What do you mean — he *was* married?'

'His wife, Phyllis, died last year,' said

189

Molly gently. 'Didn't you know?'

Rosemary stood with her mouth open.

'Phyllis died?' she repeated in a trance.

'Yes. I'll tell you all about it one day but right now I must get going,' Molly said, slipping on her raincoat and hat. 'Goodbye.'

* * *

When a loud knock came at the front door next day, a vision of the unpleasant meeting with the two village ladies sprang to Rosemary's mind and she went to the door reluctantly.

She was horrified to find one of them standing there and grasped the door handle tightly.

'Good morning, Mrs Whittington.' She had managed to remember the constable's wife.

'I've come to apologise, Miss Shepherd.'

Rosemary could see the woman was

ill at ease by the way she kept trying to push her hair back.

'Oh, Mrs Whittington, I ought to apologise to you, too, for shutting the door on you!'

They were soon laughing at the previous confrontation and Rosemary felt she was making a friend.

'We didn't know how much work you've been doing — and looking after the children so well. Dulcie Richardson was most distressed when she heard how mistaken we were about you. And Bill Clatterdove says you've saved his grandson from prison.'

Embarrassed to receive such praise, Rosemary felt her cheeks glow.

'Come in and have a cup of tea,' she said opening the door.

'Just a quick one then. And may I see the babies? I do so love babies.'

'I'm sure Dianne will love to show them off. They're adorable!'

The fact that Miss Fairclough hadn't come with Mrs Whittington didn't surprise Rosemary. Her type didn't apologise. But Rosemary was sure that next time they met, she would be more agreeable.

Dianne was proud to show Thelma Whittington her babies, and Thelma enthused over the little ones, who had grown considerably in the weeks they'd been home.

'You must join the village Women's Institute, Rosemary,' said Thelma as they drank a cup of tea in the kitchen a little later. 'We do much more than make jam, as most people think.'

'Yes, yes, I will.' Rosemary said. 'The Morton family are leaving next week and I'll miss them all. And Nicky is going back to his home in Holland tomorrow. So I'll have plenty of time on my hands.'

She didn't say how much she dreaded the thought of being all alone in an empty house.

Well, she'd have the cat, she thought sadly.

★ ★ ★

They had to say goodbye to Nicky first.

'He's almost grown out of the new clothes I got him.' Dianne sounded wistful. 'Even though I thought I'd got him some that were too big.'

'We've had fun playing together,' David said. 'I'll miss him.'

'We all will,' said Rosemary, carefully packing a basket of eggs for him to take home.

'Look after my hens, please, Rosemary?' Nicky asked anxiously, and smiled when she said she was keen to. Rosemary had become quite attached to Wilhelmina, Beatrix, Lysbeth and Juliana. And having the fresh eggs was wonderful.

Nicky told her that when he became a rich farmer, he would come back to see them all.

The Dutch boy kissed everyone — including the twins, the cat, and the hens — and said a polite thank you, before getting into the Red Cross car waiting to take him down to the ferry.

David looked glum at losing his friend.

'I hope he won't be too hungry before he gets home,' put in Susan anxiously.

David comforted his sister.

'Rosemary made him a pile of egg and cress sandwiches, and she put some rock cakes in his basket.'

Dianne was tearful. 'I never thought when we agreed to have a Dutch boy for a spell, that I'd become so attached to him. He's grown so tall and handsome since he's been with us.'

Rosemary wiped a tear from her eye. 'Come on,' she said, as the car disappeared out of view, 'I think we could all do with a rock cake to cheer us up.'

★ ★ ★

It took some getting used to, not having Nicky around. He'd become so much a part of the family during his stay with them.

194

Rosemary was delighted to have his hens and thought she couldn't have wished for a better leaving present from him.

'Hens are great fun to keep,' she told the family at supper that night. 'And I'll have plenty of time to look after them as well as Nicky would have done.'

'Now, you two, if you've finished, off to bed,' said Dianne. 'Rosemary and I have a lot of packing to do.'

Rosemary's face fell. Packing meant the family were due to leave soon — and she felt sad every time she thought about that.

Presents All Round

With the day of the Mortons' departure creeping ever closer, Rosemary was busier than ever. Bulging suitcases and boxes were beginning to clutter the hall, and young David and Susan were excited at the thought of a new house.

'I don't know what I'll do without you and Molly to help with the babies,' said Dianne, with a sigh and a frown as she surveyed the growing pile of luggage.

'You'll manage fine. And David and Susan are eager to lend a hand,' Rosemary replied.

'Thanks to you — you've worked wonders with them.'

'Oh no, they're good children. You and Michael have a lovely family.'

'Don't look so wistful, Rosemary,' Dianne said quietly. 'You'll soon have your own family.'

Rosemary closed her mouth tightly. She would love to have a family of her own, but with Rob gone, Dennis a dead loss — and John . . .

She swallowed hard. It had occurred to her that if John hadn't told her he was free to marry again, it could only mean that he didn't want anything more than a friendship with her. So that was another hope gone.

So what chance did she have of marrying and having a family?

'I suppose I'll have to go out dancing to meet someone,' Rosemary said, thinking out loud.

Dianne looked surprised. 'Mike and I thought you had a boyfriend.'

'Oh no,' said Rosemary, thinking of Dennis Painter. 'He asked me, but I'd never marry him.'

Dianne was puzzled. She'd been under the impression that Rosemary was very fond of John Hythe.

'Why not?' she asked.

'He's not right. Not right for me at all.'

Dianne looked disappointed. 'Well, no man is perfect,' she said slowly, thinking of John's physical handicap.

'Anyway, I've nothing suitable to wear for going out,' Rosemary said, looking down at her tweed skirt and remembering how scathing Dennis had been about her style of dress. 'He said I could look a real smasher in the right clothes. Cheeky of him, wasn't it, when clothes are so hard to get?'

'I'll say it was!' What a strange thing for John to say, Dianne thought. The doctor was usually such a gentleman. Always kind.

'Well, I assure you,' said Rosemary, 'any possible romance between us is over.' She'd be pleased never to see Dennis again.

'When we're gone, you'll have the time to reconsider,' Dianne said, smiling.

Susan came rushing in at that moment. 'Rosemary, can I take your fairy cycle?'

Glad to have the chance to get away

from talking about her love life, Rosemary answered, 'Of course you may. I'm much too big for it now. I'm glad you'll be able to look after it — and Rose can have it when she's older, can't she?'

'And you've grown out of your dolls now, too, haven't you?' Susan asked innocently.

'Now don't be greedy,' Dianne scolded. 'Perhaps Rosemary will want her dolls for her own little girls when she has them.'

Susan took Rosemary's hand and gazed imploringly up at her. 'May I take just one — or two?'

'I'm sure I can spare one or two.' Rosemary looked appealingly at Dianne for her agreement.

Dianne laughed. 'Very well. But show Rosemary which ones you'd like.'

Susan nodded, and said, 'And David would like the Snakes and Ladders and some books.'

'Oh, dear,' said Dianne, looking at Rosemary apologetically. 'As if you haven't done enough for us already.'

'It's only fair for David to have something too,' said Rosemary. 'Let him bring me the things he wants, then I'll decide what he can have.'

★   ★   ★

In general the post had been bringing Rosemary news from her Wren friends, but that day a postal order had arrived from Dulcie Richardson for the domestic work she'd done for her.

Rosemary made up her mind in an instant.

'I'm going shopping in Exeter tomorrow,' she told Dianne. 'Will you manage on your own?'

'Yes, of course,' said Dianne. 'Lucky you, getting a shopping trip. I'd like to get some clothes for the children — they're all growing so fast.'

'Come with me,' Rosemary offered impulsively. 'We can go in my car. I don't think I've forgotten how to drive

— and John left me a full tank of petrol.'

'David and Susan will be in school, but I can't, with the twins.'

'I'm sure Mrs Richardson would come up and look after the babies for a few hours — she's brought up a family. And Molly could pop in and check they were OK.'

'Would she?' Dianne looked hopeful.

'I'll trot down and ask her,' said Rosemary.

Just then the phone rang. She answered it to find that it was John Hythe, wondering if she would like to go out for a meal on Friday night, after the Mortons had left.

Still in the hall sorting out some things in one of her bags, Dianne overheard some of the conversation.

'Yes, thank you, John,' Rosemary was saying, 'I'd like that very much.'

Dianne hid her smile.

Rosemary popped quickly down to the village to thank Dulcie for the money and to ask her if she would be able to come up the next day and look after the twins for a few hours.

'I'd love to,' said Dulcie.

'You're a gem. I'll fetch you and Hetty in the car at about ten-thirty tomorrow morning.'

★ ★ ★

It was a treat for Rosemary and Dianne to be out shopping in Exeter. They even had time for a quick coffee break when they arrived.

'These synthetic meringues don't taste anywhere as good as they were before the war,' said Rosemary, looking at the white crumbs on her plate with distaste and wishing she hadn't been tempted to buy one. 'They leave a horrid taste in the mouth. Heaven knows what they put in them.'

'Your rock cakes are much nicer,' Dianne commented.

Having lots to do between them, they decided to split up to shop and arranged a time and place to meet up again afterwards.

As Rosemary went about her business, she felt elated with a sense of freedom.

It was, she realised, the freedom Dennis Painter had meant that day when she'd left the WRNS, when he had said that she was getting away from other people telling her what to do.

At that time she hadn't appreciated what he'd meant, but now she strode happily down the High Street, thrilled to feel that her life was just starting again, with all the opportunities and joys it offered.

No longer did she think the Mortons' departure was going to be a disaster for her. It had been lovely having them there and getting to know them when she had first arrived home, but now she felt ready to say goodbye to them and to begin to make her own life.

Meeting up with Dianne later she exclaimed, 'My goodness, Dianne, just look at all those packages!'

Dianne laughed. 'I must say I'm glad

I don't have to go down to the bus station and try to get on a bus with this lot.'

Rosemary helped to carry some of the packages and they soon bundled them into the car and set off for home. It had been a successful day all round.

★ ★ ★

Two days later, they had a little get-together to mark the Mortons' leaving. Rosemary was amazed to find how many people had been invited to tea.

'Are you sure you'll be able to feed that lot?' she asked with a worried look on her face.

'Just about,' said Dianne, smiling.

Because the other downstairs rooms were still waiting to be cleaned and aired, the guests all crowded into the kitchen. The children helped to bring in chairs from all over the house so that everyone could be seated.

'I love parties,' said David, munching

his third sandwich.

'So do I.' Susan said. 'When are we going to get our presents, Mum?'

'Hush!' said her mother.

They enjoyed the chicken Mr Hunt had provided. It had been roasted and allowed to get cold then sliced up in fresh bread sandwiches, with some of Thelma Whittington's homemade chutney. Afterwards, a huge plate of Rosemary's rock cakes was passed round — and Rosemary was proud to notice that they disappeared very quickly. Her cooking had improved, there was no doubt about that!

As she sat back for a few moments, she looked round at all the people she'd got to know over the past few months.

How could she ever have thought that she would be lonely when the Mortons left, with all these people in her life — people she hadn't even realised had become part of her life.

She had Dulcie Richardson, Bill Clatterdove, Mr Hunt at the farm and young Jimmy, Sid delivering the milk, and Molly, the district nurse — and that was before she joined the Women's Institute with Mrs Whittington. And with John Hythe too . . .

Goodness me, Miss Rosemary Shepherd, she thought, you've wormed your way into village life all right — and you hadn't even realised it!

Thelma was delighted to be cuddling baby Nicholas, while Dulcie held baby Rose. David was sharing his fourth sandwich with Hetty, who snapped the pieces up and licked her lips long afterwards.

Matilda the cat decided to curl up on Rosemary's knee and as she stroked the soft fur, Rosemary almost fell asleep with contentment.

It was a nudge at her elbow that woke her up. There was Susan with a wide smile on her pretty little face.

'This is for you, Rosemary,' the child said, thrusting a big parcel at her.

Matilda was none too pleased at being disturbed and sprang lightly off Rosemary's lap.

Slightly embarrassed to think they had got her a present, Rosemary smiled.

'What is this, Susan? Another hen?'

'No,' said Susan, shaking her curls. 'It's — '

'Don't tell her!' David shouted.

The little girl leaned forward and whispered in Rosemary's ear, 'It's a present. But I can't tell you what it is — because I don't know! Mum got it for you.'

Rosemary probed the soft package. She couldn't even begin to guess what it might be.

She realised everyone was looking at her, waiting for her to open her parcel. So she did.

Inside the paper was a soft wool twinset, a pretty cream-coloured jumper and cardigan to match, and there was also a crimson-coloured skirt *and* a pair of nylon stockings.

'Oh! What bliss!' murmured Rosemary, holding up her garments with as much joy as Nicky had when he'd got his new clothes.

The skirt was styled in the very latest fashionable New Look, and used far more fabric than the skirts women had worn during the war.

Rosemary gulped, overcome with emotion.

'Dianne, I just don't know what to say . . . '

'Well, I'd like to say you deserve the present, Rosemary, and I hope they fit you nicely. Everyone contributed some clothing coupons,' said Dianne, smiling.

Rosemary looked around the room with glazed eyes, hearing murmurs of approval.

'It's so kind of you all. Thank you, everyone,' she said.

The chorus back astounded her: 'Thank *you*, Rosemary, for all you've done for us.'

Everyone laughed and clapped.

'Any more rock cakes left?' David asked.

'You're getting as bad as Nicky,'

grumbled his mother as she tousled his hair.

'I'm a growing lad,' retorted David with a grin.

Few people noticed John Hythe slip into the room and grab a cup of tea and the last chicken sandwich before it was fed to Hetty.

With a shortage of dress materials, and prices high, he'd made a significant contribution to Rosemary's present.

Soon he was limping away, pleased to have seen the look of surprise and delight on Rosemary's face. He hadn't been able to stay long — he was a busy doctor with work to do — but at least he'd been there to share in that special moment when everyone let Rosemary know how much she had come to mean to them.

He left with a broad smile that matched Rosemary's. Pity there had been no more of those excellent chicken sandwiches. However, he *had* managed to pocket a rock cake. And there was always Friday evening to look forward to . . .

Rosemary had, of course, bought some leaving gifts for the children. Toys were very hard to find in the shops, but in a secondhand shop in Exeter she'd discovered a boxed racing car game for David, which thrilled him to bits, and a small bicycle bell for Susan, which the little girl couldn't wait to be fitted on to her fairy cycle. Two old silver rattles with tiny bells on them were perfect for the twins once Rosemary had washed and cleaned them carefully.

Dianne was overjoyed with her almost-new leather gloves.

'Just what I need,' she exclaimed. 'I hear it can be pretty cold up north.'

A Memorable Evening

How still the house seemed without the calls and cries of the children! No running feet along the upstairs landing — no voices clamouring for this and that. The kitchen wasn't filled with the delicious aromas of Dianne's cooking. And, of course, Nicky wasn't there any more, to feed the hens.

Seated in front of her dressing-table mirror, brushing her hair, preparing to go out for the evening with John, however, Rosemary felt serene.

More than serene. Was she happy?

Yes, she decided she was. She could never entirely overcome the tragedy war had brought to her life — the death of her parents and sister, the loss of her beloved Rob.

Yet, despite this sadness, she considered the restarting of her life after her time in the WRNS had been a success.

She had helped bring to justice the black market thieves, who had been jailed, and she had helped set young Jimmy Clatterdove on a better road than the one he had been following, and he was well placed learning to farm the land.

Now that the Mortons had gone and she looked back on their time together, she felt satisfied that their stay had been a worthwhile experience for her. She'd heard they were doing well up north.

'They certainly taught me a thing or two,' she thought with a chuckle, slipping on her new twinset.

When it came to putting on her jewellery, she struggled to close the clasp of the pearl necklace around her slender neck. She wasn't used to wearing finery like this.

Before putting on her charm bracelet, she examined each charm, remembering how she'd collected them. Mum had given her most of them as birthday and Christmas presents. But Belinda had saved her pocket money to buy her the pixie . . .

She'd been lucky to have such a wonderful family.

She regarded herself in the mirror. 'You're no great beauty, Miss Shepherd,' she told herself with a wry grin. 'Or particularly skilled at anything — except radar!'

She had to admit, though, that she was becoming quite knowledgeable about housekeeping. There was a good job ahead of her, too, being paid for doing other people's housework.

'It's not a job that would suit everyone,' she thought. 'I suppose a lot of women are more ambitious than I am. But all I want is . . .'

What was it she really wanted?

She was an old-fashioned type of girl, she decided. To have a new family to look after — a family of her own — would be her dearest wish, but it was unlikely to happen.

She smiled, satisfied that she was being realistic about herself.

'You've a lot to be thankful for,' she went on lecturing herself. 'You're fit and well, have good friends, affectionate pets, and you have a lovely old house to live in. Wartime hardships are fading away and the future looks rosy — '

A sharp rap at the door made her jump.

'Heavens!' she exclaimed. 'That must be John, and I've not even finished dressing!'

Scrambling to find her shoes, she realised she'd only put one stocking on!

The knock came again. She would have to go down and let him in.

She tore down the stairs and opened the front door. When she saw John, an involuntary gasp escaped her lips.

'What's the matter?' he asked, surprised.

'You! You look . . . incredibly smart.' And handsome, she might have added.

He smiled and brushed his jacket. 'I'm glad I pass muster. I only hope I don't smell too much of mothballs. My housekeeper's a terror for distributing them everywhere.'

Rosemary smiled. 'It's not just your suit,' she said.

He rubbed his smooth chin. 'Ah, yes, I managed to find time to go to the barber too.'

She laughed. 'Come in before you impress me even more.'

As he limped after her into the hall, she moved towards the stairs. Stopping by the newel post she turned and said, 'As you can see, I'm not quite ready, I haven't got any shoes on — '

He chuckled. 'I had noticed. But I also noticed how lovely you look.'

Shyly embarrassed, she gave a twirl in her full skirt.

'Why thank you, kind sir. But I haven't any evening shoes and I can't decide which of the few pairs of shoes I do have, I should wear.'

'You've had all day to decide — what have you been doing with yourself?' he teased.

'I know it's no excuse, but not being busy is quite time consuming! I fed the hens — and Matilda. Emptied and filled the range with coke. I did a quick tidy up for Dulcie Richardson — but Bill Clatterdove needs a skip to deal with all his rubbish!'

'That I can well believe. Hurry up or we'll miss the — '

Rosemary was already running up the stairs to disappear into her room where she scurried around to find some shoes and evening bag. A dab of lipstick and she would be ready. But her hand trembled a little as she tried to imagine what he had been about to say when he had said they might miss something . . .

Did he have something up his sleeve?

'I decided on my most comfortable shoes,' she said apologetically, coming downstairs a few minutes later. 'They're not really suitable for evening wear, so don't look at them too closely, will you?'

'I promise — if you don't look at my feet, either,' he said with a chuckle, looking down at his shoe and boot.

★ ★ ★

It was a smooth run into Exeter and didn't take long. They parked outside a cinema — and to Rosemary's distress, she realised it was the cinema where her family had been killed, now rebuilt.

'John,' she whispered, 'I — I don't think I want to go in here.'

'I thought you might say that — and believe me, I'm not trying to upset you.' His voice was gentle. 'But I've heard the film is very good. I'd love to see it. And I think you'd like it too.'

'John, I just don't think I can . . .'

He sat quietly, his hand covering hers very gently.

She had to decide. She knew he wouldn't force her to go. Perhaps it was his way of helping her to overcome her pain? It wasn't as if he didn't understand her reluctance. She was sure he'd suffered his own share of unpleasant wartime experiences and had his own painful memories to blot out.

She'd also heard that some very entertaining films were being made at the Ealing Studios. Perhaps she could make the effort to overcome her fear and go?

'OK,' she said, suddenly deciding. 'Let's go.'

They did enjoy the film very much and she was glad they'd gone in. But the laughter died on their lips when they got outside the cinema — to find that John's new car had been stolen!

It was a horrid shock for him, but Rosemary admired John's calmness. After informing the police, he insisted they continued with their plans, and they took a taxi to the city restaurant where he had booked a table.

Their talk flowed freely over the excellent meal. Being old friends, they could talk about anything, even their most intimate feelings.

'I find it hard to forget Ron,' Rosemary explained. 'I loved him so much.'

'And you always will,' John added. 'I know Phyllis will always be in my heart.'

There was a bond between them, a shared understanding because they had each lost a loved one.

'But time heals the body — and the mind, too,' John said. 'We can and should move on.'

'Oh, I think I have. I've quite settled down at home now.' Rosemary smiled. 'I'd say I've carved myself a very comfortable niche.'

He grinned. 'So I've noticed.'

Rosemary sipped her wine.

'I admire you. You've had so many hard knocks since the war started. And yet you're still . . . '

'Yes?'

But she couldn't tell him he was loveable, could she?

' . . . able to overcome them,' she substituted, looking at him intently across the candle-lit table.

John looked straight back at her.

'So have you,' he said, softly.

'But this latest blow — losing your car — that's hard,' she said sympathetically.

Dabbing his mouth with his table napkin, John looked into her eyes with a touch of merriment.

'It's not the last blow,' he said.

'What do you mean?'

'I mean, we're never going to find a taxi to take us all the way home. We'll have to walk.'

Rosemary chuckled. 'It's just as well I'm not wearing those high-heeled evening shoes, after all, then.'

'Well,' he said, 'it was all part of a plan, actually. When I saw your sensible shoes, I reckoned a healthy ex-Wren wouldn't mind a six-mile walk.' His eyes twinkled and she couldn't help laughing.

They left the restaurant in the best of spirits.

They were fortunate that the night held a clear moon in the cloudless sky and the exercise of walking kept them warm.

The road was empty of traffic, which made the walk more pleasant, and an owl kept them company for several miles, hooting periodically as they walked along.

'Need a rest?' John asked her after about three miles.

'I'm OK,' she replied. 'How about you? Does your foot bother you?'

'Which one?'

Rosemary giggled. No matter what difficulties he had, John retained the old Navy spirit of making a joke of things.

There were a lot of nice things about their walk, too. She spotted snowdrops and primroses in the hedgerows. Fat buds were forming on the branches of the trees. Signs of new life were everywhere . . . Spring's glory was about to unfold.

At one point a trail of deer trotted across the road in front of them, some no bigger than large dogs.

'This is magical,' she said. 'I'll never forget this midnight walk with you. Of course, you're used to being out at night visiting patients so this evening probably won't strike you as being anything special.'

'Rosemary,' he said, coming closer to her and taking her hand, 'this evening will always be very special for me too — although it's not working out quite as I'd planned.'

She felt him squeeze her hand and a shiver of excitement ran through her.

'I don't mind the long tramp home,' she said with a laugh, and it was true.

'I just don't know when I'll get the opportunity to take you out again,' he went on. 'Although you may say 'never again' after this fiasco!'

'Oh, John, it's not your fault your car has been stolen.'

'True. I suppose I'll have to try to get hold of that Jeep again.'

'You don't have to — you can use my car. Really it's our car now — you use it as much as I do!'

'That's kind of you,' he murmured.

They both turned at the sound of a clanking milk float behind them. It was coming closer!

'Why, bless my soul, if it ain't Dr

Hythe and Miss Shepherd!'

Sid, the milkman, was amused to see the pair plodding along the road in the early hours.

'Want a lift?' he called, slowing beside them.

'We wouldn't mind,' said Rosemary gratefully.

'Hop in then,' Sid said. 'This ain't no Rolls Royce, but it'll get you there by breakfast time. You're not the first people I'll have picked up of a morning who've missed the bus home.'

Laughing, the two weary walkers squashed into the front seat of his float, and Sid trundled along to collect the next load of milk churns waiting outside a farm gate.

Sitting so close to John was comforting and cosy. As she yawned widely, he put his arm around her, and the gentle rocking of the milk-cart had soon sent her to sleep.

★ ★ ★

The sunrise was just beginning to lighten the sky when she awoke.

'I wouldn't have thought so many people would be up this early in the morning,' she remarked, recognising Jimmy biking by and giving a friendly wave.

A car approached them, Molly in her old Morris. Seeing them, she slowed, and wound down the car window for a quick word with John about the treatment of a patient.

'I called in at your lodgings, Dr Hythe, and the housekeeper said you'd been out all night.'

Molly glanced meaningfully at Rosemary, who blushed.

'I need to get to the surgery,' John said once Molly had driven off. 'A patient is waiting for urgent treatment and I have to collect my bag and the drugs I'll need.'

When John got off the float in the High Street, Rosemary did too, so they wouldn't be holding Sid up with his rounds.

Still attired in her evening wear as she was, Rosemary was aware of a few raised eyebrows and sideways glances from those who passed by. Obviously seeing her with the doctor, dressed in their best in the early hours of the morning, was a sight for speculation and would soon be all over the village!

First they were greeted by the baker boy as he wobbled by on his bike with his basket full of loaves, out on his first delivery of the day.

Next, two shop assistants saw them as they hurried to get to work on time, and then Miss Fairclough came striding past them on her morning constitutional and wished them 'Good morning' in a very loud and pointed manner.

'Let me take you home first,' said John, when Sid had driven his float away up the street.

Rosemary noticed that John was looking rather anxious and gave him a wry grin; what was the point of trying to hide from the village that they had been together all night?

No doubt people would put two and two together and make five, but there was nothing that could be done about it now.

Besides, although it was a little embarrassing, *they* both knew the truth of the situation and that was all that mattered really, when it came down to it.

'There's no need to take me home,' she protested. 'You mustn't lose any time in getting to your patient. I'll go and fetch my car and bring it to the surgery for you.'

'Well . . . ' He checked his watch, torn between what he wanted to do and his duty to his patient. 'It would be a help,' he finally agreed a little reluctantly. 'I'm sorry to put you to such trouble, though.'

'It's no trouble,' she said with another grin. 'You know I've got nothing else to do all day. It'll give me something to keep me occupied.'

He laughed, too, then shook his head

as he looked at her intently.

'My dear Rosemary, will you ever be able to forgive me for ruining what should have been an enjoyable night out?'

'It *was* a wonderful evening, John — and I know you have to put your patients' needs first.'

'So you'll accept another invitation for an evening out?' There was a hopeful look on his face.

'Like a shot,' she said, standing on tip-toes to kiss his cheek before hurrying off home to fetch the car.

John watched her go, a strange feeling in his heart. It was rather like the way he felt when he was working in his garden and came across an exquisite, unexpected flower blooming amongst a tangle of weeds.

★ ★ ★

The new National Health Service was announced on the wireless and Dr John Hythe was occupied with the changes that it would bring to his practice, so Rosemary wasn't surprised that she hadn't seen him for a week or so.

She'd had plenty to keep her busy, in any case. She had now built up a regular round of people who needed their houses cleaned or some other form of help. She enjoyed polishing windows, scrubbing floors, taking pets for walks and shopping for people who couldn't get to the shops for themselves.

And, of course, chatting! There was plenty of that to do, as many of the people lived alone and were always eager for company.

Her own house could do with a thorough spring clean, too, she decided, and set about the task with her usual determination and energy.

Before long, the downstairs rooms were cleared out, scrubbed and polished, and ready for use. But used for what? That was the question.

Should she start a bed and breakfast business? It was something she mused on from time to time. She chuckled — at least she wouldn't go short of eggs for breakfast, thanks to Nicky!

If she wanted to attract customers, though, she would have to do something with her garden, she considered, looking critically out of the kitchen window at it. There seemed to be nothing but weeds — much appreciated by the hens, of course, but a dreadful sight for everyone else.

Right, that was the next job on her list, she resolved.

She smiled to herself, remembering how unused to making decisions she'd been when she had first arrived home after leaving the Wrens. She'd certainly become much better at that over the past few months!

★　★　★

One fine spring day Rosemary stood in her garden, resplendent in her new Wellingtons on her tired feet, and ran her fingers through her hair. What on earth was she going to do with the overgrown patch? There was so much of it! And the outhouses needed attention, too.

She'd become quite good at keeping house, but, oh dear me, her huge garden was like a jungle — with a hen-coop in it!

'Need some help to tame that lot?'

The voice broke into her thoughts and she swung round to face the doctor.

'John!' She smiled delightedly at him. 'I'd be glad of some ideas. I don't know anything about gardening.'

'I'm sorry if I've neglected you, my dear. I've been so busy,' he said, bending and giving her a kiss.

'You don't have to apologise,' she said, thrilled at the kiss. 'I know a doctor's life is a busy one. Have you got a minute for a cup of tea, though?'

'Just what the doctor ordered,' he said as he came into the house.

While Rosemary took off her boots and made the tea he said, 'I've brought your car back, with my grateful thanks.'

'Lovely! That means you've managed to get another?'

'A Rover. It's second-hand, of course, but you'll enjoy a spin in it.'

Rosemary smiled as she put two cups of tea down on the table. 'I expect I will — if I'm asked.'

'Of course you will be!'

He sipped his tea, then cleared his throat a little nervously.

'Actually, I've come to ask you something else. Well, to be honest, after hearing all the village chatter, I'm going to have to ask you to save my reputation.'

She giggled, knowing that by now everyone would know about their night out together.

'What about *my* reputation?'

'Oh, naturally, yours too . . . ' he said slowly. Then he went on to explain.

'You see, my housekeeper told me some time ago that she intends to retire. I'd started looking around for somewhere else to live, but . . . '

231

'I suppose I could offer you a room here,' Rosemary put in. 'I've been thinking about starting bed and breakfast . . .'

John's face fell. 'A room?'

'Your meals would be included, of course . . .' she said, misunderstanding his disappointment.

'Of course. But I wasn't actually looking for a new landlady, Rosemary. I was about to say that I've changed my mind about looking for lodgings. I — I mean, I was hoping that I — that you — that we . . .'

Rosemary's heart leapt. Was this leading where she thought — and hoped — it was?

'John . . . ?'

He leaned forward and took her hand gently in his.

'I can't take you dancing, but I enjoy gardening and can help you get your garden ship-shape. But it's not just that, Rosemary. Whether we're gardening or feeding hens or only sitting drinking tea, I — I don't care where I am, I just like it better when you're there too.'

'I do too, John,' she whispered.

'What I'm trying to say, Rosemary, is . . . will you marry me?'

'Yes,' she said delightedly as he moved to take her in his arms. It was the easiest decision she'd ever had to make.

THE END

Warwickshire County Council

MOBILE LIBRARY SERVICE

12/11 *Knight*	P.J.	
2 7 SEP 2012		
1 8 OCT 2012		
3 1 DEC 2012		
– 3 MAY 2013		
2 1 OCT 2013		
Depton		
Chandos		
Warehouse		

This item is to be returned or renewed before the latest date above. It may be borrowed for a further period if not in demand. **To renew your books:**

- **Phone the 24/7 Renewal Line 01926 499273 or**
- **Visit www.warwickshire.gov.uk/libraries**

Discover • Imagine • Learn • *with libraries*

Warwickshire County Council

Working for Warwickshire